LORDS, LOVE & STOLEN JEWELS (BOOK 1)

LORDS, LOVE AND STOLEN JEWELS (BOOK 1)

CHARLOTTE FITZWILLIAM

HIS

LOVE

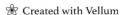

PROLOGUE

Lady Angelica Landerbelt sighed heavily to herself as yet another gentleman appeared in the gold-encrusted doorway of her drawing room, the butler announcing him with a small smile in her direction. As she sat in all her finery, she could not return the smile. Her butler, Franks, knew full well that she was finding this particular situation to be rather difficult, and he was trying his best to show *some* kind of sympathy.

Franks, whose formal manners made him perfect for his position, had been a part of her household staff for years, and Angelica had come to find him invaluable, especially after the death of her own husband, the Marquess of Landerbelt, two years ago. Franks carried himself with a confidence and dignity that caused one to know they could rely on him. The hair that he had left was dark and well kept. His head was often held high and his brown eyes were often expressionless.

"It is truly wonderful to have you back in London again, Lady Landerbelt," the new gentleman exclaimed, bowing deeply at the waist. His expensive black suit highlighted his medium build. "I do hope I am not intruding, but I simply could not wait to welcome you back to town."

Lady Landerbelt held herself demurely with her ivory skin highlighting her thin features and her chestnut curls perfectly arranged. She arched one eyebrow, wondering if the gentleman would notice the two others that were sitting in her drawing room, as well as the maid that sat in the corner, knitting busily. Angelica wanted to tell him that, yes, he was intruding—and that, in fact, all three were unwelcome given that they had not made any kind of inquiry as to whether or not she would welcome visitors during afternoon calls—but propriety forced her to remain silent.

"Lord Caversham, was it?" she murmured, as the man sat down.

"Yes, Lady Landerbelt," Lord William Caversham replied, with a small bow. "We met two nights ago at Lady Portillo's musical evening."

She vaguely remembered him, allowing her eyes to run over him as he settled himself in a ruby-red chair. He was not overly tall but with a strong frame that seemed to have to be squeezed into the chair. His shock of black hair brought an even greater shade to the dark brown of his eyes, which were darting about in an almost nervous fashion. There was a look of strength about him, with his strong jaw clenched and lips firm. Yes, she admitted to herself, he was handsome enough, but—given that she had come to London at the height of the Season—Angelica was sure she would meet a great many handsome gentlemen with nothing more than a thin veneer underneath their features.

She leaned back and took in the ornate woodwork that adorned her red velvet chair and couch, using it as a moment to take a break from conversing with the men in her presence. Glancing to her left, she could not help but feel relieved at the sight of the large grandfather clock, indicating that she only had to wait a bit longer before the time for visitors would end.

Seeing Lord Caversham look back at her expectantly, she

managed a quick smile in his direction, which he did not return. "Thank you for your kind words. I was just saying to Lord Hawthorn and Lord Porteous that I am only in London to chaperone a particular young lady—Lady Catherine Newton—who will be staying with me. Therefore, you must not hope that I will be indulging in any of society's pleasures, not when I have a young lady in my care."

The light faded in Lord Caversham's eyes as he looked back at her, forcing Angelica to hide her smile. It was clear that each and every gentleman here had come for one reason and one reason only – to ingratiate themselves with her in the hope that she might look favorably upon them and, perhaps in time, allow them to court her.

The very idea was laughable.

"But I am sure you will allow yourself one or two dances," Lord Porteous said, his voice thin and his expression dark. "After all, Lady Landerbelt, it can come as no surprise to you to know that you are much in demand at the moment."

She laughed and shook her head. "I am only in demand, Lord Porteous, because I have a vast fortune, and there are more than a few poor gentlemen who think of nothing but getting their hands on it." Laughter escaped her again as she looked at the three gentlemen in her drawing room, seeing them glancing back at one another as though they were all vastly astonished at hearing this from her. She knew that she was being rather frank with them, but having grown tired of their constant flattery and obsequiousness, she had chosen to tell them the truth in the hope that they would then choose to leave her well enough alone.

"Do not for one moment think that I have any intention of marrying again, gentlemen. I have mourned for my husband, yes, but that does not mean that a lady such as myself, with such a vast fortune as I possess, will simply throw herself headlong at the first gentleman who compliments her." She tossed her head, her laughter fading as a thin sliver of anger tugged at her heart. "No, gentlemen, I will not be looking towards matrimony. This return to London is not what you hoped for, I am sorry to say. You may attempt to pursue me as much as you wish, but I can assure you now that it will all come to naught."

Her words faded away, and Angelica lifted her head high, straightening her shoulders and ensuring she sat tall and strong, her eyes lingering on each gentleman in turn. Lord Porteous had gone puce; Lord Hawthorn appeared to be rather angry; and Lord Caversham clearly had very little idea of what to say or do, for his mouth opened and closed like a fish that had been pulled from the water.

Then, without warning, Lord Porteous got to his feet and walked away from the ornate velvet-covered chair where he had been sitting. Maneuvering around a dark wood table, he approached Lady Landerbelt and said, "I think, Lady Landerbelt, that I must excuse myself. I am afraid that I have outstayed my welcome a little, and I apologize for that."

She inclined her head, not feeling even the slightest modicum of guilt over what she had said. "Good afternoon, Lord Porteous. Thank you for taking the time to call upon me this afternoon."

"And I, too, must excuse myself," Lord Hawthorn said, as he abruptly stood. His lips were thin, and his eyes were flashing as he looked back at her, clearly rather angry with what she had explained. "I do not think I shall call again."

Angelica bit back a harsh retort, knowing that to tell him that she would not find his lack of company to be any kind of trial would be nothing more than snide.

"Good day, Lady Landerbelt," Lord Hawthorn finished, marching to the drawing-room door with Lord Porteous following close behind. "And I suppose I must thank you for your time." He did not wait for the butler to open the door but pulled it open himself, with such force that it almost banged back against the wall, making Angelica wince.

"My, my," she murmured, sitting back a little in her chair. "Lord Porteous, it seems, does not take kindly to being so rejected." She arched one brow at Lord Caversham, who was still sitting in his seat, looking somewhat stunned. "Are you about to quit the room in a similar fashion, Lord Caversham?"

He swallowed hard and looked at her with wide eyes, shaking his head just a little.

"I see," she murmured, a small smile tugging at her lips. "Then you do not take offense at my frank speech, Lord Caversham. Perhaps that is a good thing."

Lord Caversham goggled at her for another few moments, clearly at a loss for what to say, only for the drawing-room door to open and the maid to step inside with the tea tray.

"Now, you see," Angelica said grandly, as the maid set the tray down on the table just to her left. "You shall have tea and cakes; we shall talk for a few minutes; and then we may part just as amiably as we can. What say you to that, Lord Caversham?"

He shook his head, his eyes darting from the tea tray to her face and back again, giving him something of an uncomfortable air. Angelica frowned, pouring the tea regardless as Lord Caversham continued to sit in complete silence, his hands now twisting in his lap.

Something was a little off, here, she was sure of it. But what?

"Lord Caversham, is something the matter?" she asked, choosing to be direct. "You appear to be rather agitated."

Lord Caversham's eyes shot to hers, his lips thinning.

"Please *do* speak plainly," Angelica added, handing him a cup of milky tea. "I cannot abide anything else." She looked back at him pointedly, picking up her own cup and saucer and taking the tiniest of sips, all the while waiting for Lord Caversham to speak.

"Lady Landerbelt, I am not here to attempt to court you."

Her expression was something between astonishment and mirth. "Well, that is good of you to say, Lord Caversham."

"I did not know who else to turn to," he confessed, setting the cup and saucer back down on the table with a lack of finesse that made the china rattle rather dangerously. "But then I heard that you returned to London, and I had to hope that you might be willing to help her."

"*Her?*"

Lord Caversham looked even more uncomfortable. "My younger sister."

Now thoroughly confused, Angelica closed her eyes for a moment, drew in a long breath and settled her shoulders. "You need to be a little more precise, Lord Caversham," she said firmly, opening her eyes. "What is it about your sister?"

Lord Caversham cleared his throat, looking back at her steadily. "She has been out for two years, Lady Landerbelt, and I have been hoping that a good match will soon come her way. My sister is as refined as can be, with grace, elegance, and a good deal of our mother's beauty." He hesitated, looking away for a moment. "However, she has recently been rather shunned from society, and it is in this that I pray you can help." He looked almost desperate, his eyes filled with worry and concern over his younger sister, and Angelica felt her own heart soften in response.

"It speaks well of your heart that you care so much for your sister," she admitted, slowly tipping her head to the side so as to regard him a little more carefully. "I must ask, however, whether it is that you wish her to be gone from your home so that you might have it entirely to yourself? I know that a great many gentlemen left with the care of their sisters or the like often find them to be a source of annoyance."

"No, indeed, I do not!" Lord Caversham exclaimed, his eyes widening. "My sister is the dearest creature in this world, and I cannot see what is going on and do nothing! She is being made the scapegoat, and unless I find someone to help her, then she will remain a spinster for the rest of her days, shunned by society, which has already decided that she is guilty."

This made Angelica frown, finding that her head was already beginning to ache with all that Lord Caversham said, her eyes taking him in entirely. He appeared to be very much in earnest, although still rather nervous given how he twisted his fingers together in his lap, his tea now untouched and cooling on the table.

She sighed inwardly, trying to keep a small smile on her face.

"Lord Caversham, again, you are not being clear. What is it that your sister is innocent of?"

"Theft!" Lord Caversham exclaimed, gesticulating wildly as though she ought to have guessed. "There has been a spate of thefts these last two weeks, and for whatever reason, my sister has been made out to be the thief when I know it could not have been her. She did not take those jewels!"

"Then why has she been accused?"

Lord Caversham swallowed and sat back in his chair, his face now a mask as he attempted to hide his true emotions from her. "Because two gentlemen supposedly saw her with the jewels at two different events," he said dully.

Angelica shook her head and sighed, seeing Lord Caversham's distress and growing concerned that the simple truth might be that his sister *had* indeed stolen the jewels and that, for whatever reason, Lord Caversham could not accept that.

"I know that you removed yourself successfully from another, rather similar situation, and I thought that you might be able to help my sister," Lord Caversham finished, sounding desperate. "If you do not, I fear that she will shrink back into the shadows and then become nothing more than a whisper – a memory, if you will – of the lady she once was. I cannot allow that to happen."

Pressing her lips together, Angelica thought for a moment. It was quite true that she had, indeed, managed to remove herself from supposed guilt that was mounting on her shoulders, ending up directing it towards the one person who had, in fact, been responsible, but that did not mean that she wished to do it again.

"And has it never occurred to you that your sister might have done what she is accused of?" she asked gently, leaning a little further forward in her seat. "Lord Caversham, I can understand that this must be very difficult for you but—"

"I *know* she did not take those pieces!" he exclaimed, surprising her with his fervor. "She has no need to! She is beautiful and wealthy, coming from a good title and family and with a large dowry for when she marries. What possible reason could she have for stealing such items?"

It was, Angelica had to admit, something of a sticking point.

"If you would just meet her, just speak to her, then I would be more than grateful," Lord Caversham continued fervently. "I will have no expectations, Lady Landerbelt, other than that. Just to discuss the matter with her?"

Sighing, Angelica found herself nodding despite her misgivings. "I do not wish to raise your hopes, Lord Caversham. I have more than enough to do this Season, what with trying to help my niece make her debut in society, and on top of which, I can give you no guarantee that I will be in any way helpful, should I decide to look into the matter further."

A long sigh came from him and, to her surprise, he ducked his head for a moment as though threatened by tears. She did not speak but waited for him to raise his head, which he did only a few moments later. She found her heart filling with sympathy and compassion for him, aware that he truly did care for his sister and her reputation. That was enough to speak to her of his true character, she realized, her lips curving into a gentle smile as he began to thank her profusely.

"I have not done anything yet, Lord Caversham," she reminded him, as he bent over her hand. "But I will listen to your sister, of course. Might you bring her here in two days' time for afternoon tea?"

He nodded, his dark features suddenly lighting with a small flicker of hope. "I will. You are very good, Lady Landerbelt. I do not think I shall ever be able to thank you."

Angelica smiled and nodded, her eyes lingering on him as he walked towards the door. Whatever had she gotten herself into?

1

"And how is my dear brother?"

Miss Catherine Newton looked up with her bright green eyes, and she saw her aunt, Lady Angelica Landerbelt, pass by her and playfully lift up one of her blond curls as she reached for the tea. Lady Landerbelt poured them both another cup, which was difficult to drink when Catherine was in the middle of a rather difficult piece of embroidery. The two had been sitting in comfortable silence in Lady Landerbelt's drawing room, enjoying the warm fire that the maid had just recently stoked.

"He is well, Aunt," she replied, thinking fondly of her father. "And rather glad that you are neither in jail nor hanging from the gallows!"

Lady Landerbelt laughed, her eyes sparkling. "I am sure my brother never once believed that I killed my dear John."

"No, he did not," Catherine replied firmly. "He always assured both myself and Rodger that you were quite innocent."

Her aunt's laughter faded, only to be replaced by a look of fondness. "Dear George always did have my best in mind."

Viscount George Higgs, Catherine's father, had always been

careful to look out for his younger sister despite the large number of years between them, which meant that, growing up, Catherine had spent a great deal of time with her aunt and had grown rather fond of her. Even though there was a good ten years between them, Catherine had found her aunt to be more of a friend than anything else, which made her willingness to chaperone Catherine during the London season even sweeter.

"Your father was always a good man," Angelica murmured, lifting her cup of tea to her lips. "I can still remember his wedding day."

Catherine smiled. "You must have been quite young at the time."

"I was twelve years old, I think," came the reply. "Your father married young, just as he was expected to do given that he was to carry on the title one day. I think he was but twenty!"

Catherine smiled to herself, remembering her beautiful mother with a great deal of affection. "I think he loved my mother from the moment he set eyes on her."

"I am certain he did," Angelica agreed, with a small, sad smile. "Rodger was produced first, within a year of marriage, and then you the year afterward. My goodness, I have memories of holding you in my arms, declaring to my brother that you were the loveliest child I had ever seen – and now look at you!"

There was a slight sadness in Catherine's heart as she accepted the glowing compliments from her aunt, wishing that it had been her mother here with her, bringing her to London and chaperoning her through the difficulties that came with entering into the London society.

"She would have been very proud," Angelica said softly, as though she knew what Catherine was thinking. "How long has it been now?"

"Five years," Catherine replied, feeling the ache in her throat build slowly. "I miss her every day." Her mother had succumbed to a fever, leaving this world less than a week after she had become ill. It had all been so sudden, so utterly devastating, that Catherine sometimes still felt as though she had not quite managed to accept it had ever really happened. Her father had become a shadow of himself for some time, and it had only been the death of Angelica's husband, the Marquess of Landerbelt, that had brought him back to life. He had hurried to her side, helped her defend herself when accusations of murder had been laid before her and had been protective and determined when it came to clearing her name.

"Do you still miss Lord Landerbelt, Aunt?"

Catherine watched as Angelica looked back at her, perhaps a little surprised by the question, only to shrug and look away.

"I did not ever love him in the same way that your mother and father loved one another," she replied softly, in a voice that was both thin and fatigued at the same time. "We did care for one another, I think, but there was never an ounce of true affection in terms of loving one another. I lost a very dear friend, and that tore me apart, but there was nothing more to it than that. To be so accused, however, took a great deal of my strength from me and had your father not appeared to aid me in it, I do not think I would have been able to free myself from their accusations."

Catherine shook her head fervently. "You were the one to discover the truth, Aunt," she said firmly. "Father has always said that he did nothing but help you dig through the clues until you came upon the truth. You have a sharp mind, I know, and you ought not to put your own skills to one side as you are doing."

Her aunt laughed, brightening the atmosphere in the room. "You are very kind, my dear niece. Let us say that I was very glad to be able to point out to the authorities that my husband had, unbeknownst to me, a mistress who was rather disgruntled with his lack of affection towards her of late." A flash of pain crossed her face, even though she smiled. "It did not take long for them to find the evidence they needed."

Catherine smiled back, aware that her aunt had not found the revelation about her husband's mistress easy in any way. She had never wanted to ask Angelica about it, and on seeing the moment of pain in her expression, she tucked away the rest of her questions on the matter. It was in the past, and as her aunt poured yet more tea, she realized the past was where she ought to leave it.

"Now, I do not want you to think that I will do to you what occurred for me," Angelica began, as though they were starting a whole new conversation. "I will not simply find you a good match and expect you to wed him just because he is a suitable gentleman. No, indeed! You shall consider your heart and consider the man and then make your decision."

A smile crossed Catherine's face. "That is very kind of you, Aunt, although I believe my father was hoping for precisely the opposite!"

Angelica snorted in derision, shaking her head. "Men are very strange, are they not? Your father found a deep, abiding love in his marriage to your mother and yet hopes that you will simply marry someone deemed suitable by me! Whereas he knows that I, who married for practicality's sake, was left torn apart by the revelations of the mistress despite the fact that there was never any love between us." She shook her head again, adding a dash of milk to her tea, clearly a little rattled. "That will not be what will happen to you, Catherine, for I will not allow it. You will find yourself a suitable gentleman whom your heart holds some affection for – an affection he must return, of course!"

"Of course," Catherine echoed, trying not to laugh.

"No matter how many Seasons it takes!" her aunt exclaimed, her eyes dancing. "Do you hear me? You are to return to

London, year after year, until we have finally found you the right gentleman."

Unable to contain her mirth, Catherine let her peals of laughter echo around the room, picturing herself and her aunt as old ladies of quality, still desperately seeking the "right gentleman" for Catherine's hand in marriage.

"I do hope it will not take all that long, Aunt," she managed to say, regaining a little of her composure. "Besides which, do you not have any intentions of your own as regards to marriage?"

The laughter died in Angelica's eyes almost at once, bringing Catherine a degree of solemnity that had not been there before.

"No, indeed," her aunt replied quickly. "No, Catherine, I have no intention of marrying again. Certainly not in the near future, at least. I have more than enough money of my own to keep me in very good comfort for the rest of my days should I wish it, thanks to the will my late husband left, and therefore I have no need to seek another husband."

Worried that she'd managed to insult her aunt, Catherine tried to smile, her fingers knotting together in her lap. "I did not mean to pry, Aunt. I do apologize if I brought you any distress with my questions."

Her aunt smiled, breaking the tension. "Not in the least, my dear. It is a fair question but, as I said only yesterday to the gentlemen who decided to hound me here in my own home, I have no intention of doing anything other than chaperone you this season. As well as, perhaps, helping a lady I have yet to meet." This last sentence was said with a slight frown appearing between Angelica's brows, making Catherine sit up a little more, discarding her embroidery.

"What do you mean, Aunt?" she asked, lifting one eyebrow. "Helping a lady you have not met?"

Lady Landerbelt sighed, her dark brown tresses bouncing as

she shook her head. "I am not sure I will be able to do anything, for perhaps she is guilty, but her brother was so very eager that I should help her that I could not help but agree to meet her."

"Meet who?" Catherine asked, her anticipation growing. "And what did she supposedly do?"

Her aunt sighed heavily. "I am not yet sure, Catherine. Something about stealing some jewels from various homes, which apparently two gentlemen witnessed at different times. The brother of this accused lady is determined that she did not do it and came to ask me for help, given that otherwise, his sister will be shunned from society."

"And you agreed?" Catherine asked hopefully. "I do so hope you said you would offer her your aid, Aunt. After all, you were in the very same situation yourself – albeit a little more serious crime."

She waited with breathless anticipation as Lady Landerbelt sighed again and looked at her with a slightly wry smile.

"I have said I will meet the girl, that is all," she said, whilst Catherine beamed with delight. "She and her brother, Lord Caversham, are to come to tea tomorrow, although there is no need for you to attend, my dear. I am sure that you would prefer to take a walk in town, perhaps to find a new ribbon or pair of gloves?"

Gasping, Catherine stared back at her aunt for a moment, dumbstruck, only to see her aunt laughing quietly.

"You know me too well, Aunt, to know that I would wish to be left out of anything of interest," she said, shaking her finger at her aunt. "Of course I do not wish to go into town and find a new ribbon! I would much prefer to meet this lady and listen to what she has to say. That is, of course, so long as you do not mind?"

Her aunt waved a hand. "Of course I do not mind. In fact, it might be rather beneficial to have you there listening to her. We can discuss it afterward and see what we each think, for I will not make any decisions until I meet the lady, talk with her, and then spend some time considering it all. You can help me in that, if you wish it. I know that you have a sharp mind and that you are not *particularly* inclined towards fripperies or the like."

Catherine grinned. "No, indeed, I am much too sensible for that – much to father's despair." She chuckled, as her aunt threw her a knowing look, excitement winding its way through her. "I would be very glad to meet this lady and her brother, Aunt Angelica. When did you say they were coming?"

Her aunt chuckled quietly. "Tomorrow, for afternoon tea," she replied with a broad smile.

"Wonderful," Catherine murmured, her eyes bright. "I can hardly wait."

2

Having just stepped into the foyer of Lady Angelica Landerbelt's home, Lord Caversham could not help but chastise his younger sister—Olivia. She had been fidgeting the entire carriage ride over and had yet to still herself. "Do not look so nervous, Olivia, else Lady Landerbelt will think you guilty almost as soon as you step into the room."

Lord William Caversham took in his surroundings, noticing the details along the woodwork of Lady Landerbelt's foyer, and he tried not to grow frustrated with his younger sister, who was busy adjusting her hair, as the butler took his gloves and hat. It was quite clear that Olivia was anxious about speaking to Lady Landerbelt, but he did not want his sister to give an unfavorable impression.

"I *am* nervous, Caversham," Olivia murmured, looking up at him with hazel eyes that were filled with fright. "If Lady Landerbelt does not believe me, then I am done for. I shall have no other choice but to retire to the country and remain there for the rest of my days." Her voice cracked, her eyes glazing with tears, and once again William felt the familiar spike of sympathy rush through him.

"Do try and hold it together, Olivia," he said a little gentler. "I am sure that Lady Landerbelt will be sympathetic towards your plight. After all, did I not tell you that she was accused of something much worse—killing her husband—and she managed to find a way to prove that it was not her who had killed him?"

Olivia nodded, blinking furiously so as to clear the tears from her eyes.

"Then you need to calm yourself and speak plainly to her," William continued, offering his sister his arm. "I am here with you, just as I have always been. Tell her the truth, tell her everything, and we will pray that she might be able to help us in some way. She is the late wife of a marquess, Olivia, and even her presence by your side in the midst of society will help you. Trust me, my dear. All is not yet lost."

Olivia swallowed once, twice, and then nodded. A watery smile slipped onto her face as she lifted her chin, showing a spark of determination that he had not seen in as many weeks.

"Very good," he said, walking towards the butler who had been waiting to lead them towards the drawing room. "Nothing to be afraid of, Olivia. You have more strength in you than you know."

Walking into the drawing room, William felt his sister tense as the butler made the introductions, a little surprised to see a lady he did not recognize rise to her feet.

"Lord Caversham, thank you for coming," Lady Landerbelt began, gesturing for him to come into the room and sit down. "And it is my pleasure to make your acquaintance, Lady Olivia."

"The pleasure is mine," Olivia managed to say, her voice a little too soft but, at the very least, still audible. "Thank you for your kindness in inviting us here, Lady Landerbelt."

Lady Landerbelt smiled, but there was something calculating in her eyes, as though she were assessing Olivia in some way.

"And this, as the butler said, is my niece, Miss Catherine Newton. She is the daughter of Viscount Higgs, who is my brother, and she has come to London for the Season."

William bowed carefully, greeting the lady who was looking at him with curiosity in her green eyes, finding himself growing a little uncomfortable with just how intently the lady was studying him. It was clear that Miss Newton was eager to hear what Olivia had to say, and William had to hope that this was a good sign. As he sat down, he found his eyes drifting back towards Miss Newton, finding her to be a rather lovely looking young lady, with blonde curls piled up high on the back of her head. She had an oval face with full, pink lips and a brightness in her eyes that spoke to him of intelligence and wit. He could not remember ever seeing a debutante with such a spark about her, finding it suddenly difficult to look away.

"Well, we may as well get straight to the heart of the matter," Lady Landerbelt said, as the maids set down trays bearing all kinds of delicious-looking goodies on the table, as well as one carrying cups and a china teapot. "Lady Olivia, your brother tells me that you are innocent of these thefts, but I will tell you now that I am not inclined to believe someone based simply on what their relative might say about them."

William heard Olivia's swift intake of breath and prayed that she might keep her composure about her, turning his head away from Miss Newton and back towards his sister.

"Society thinks that you are a thief," Lady Landerbelt continued, bluntly. "Might you be able to tell me what *exactly* it is that you are accused of?"

Holding his breath, William resisted the urge to speak for his sister, forcing himself to stay stock still as she glanced over at him. Putting an encouraging smile on his face and ignoring the swirls of worry that began to race through him, he watched

Olivia closely as she looked back towards Lady Landerbelt. The silence dragged on for a few minutes, making his patience stretch so thin that it grew almost painful.

"I know this must be very difficult for you, Lady Olivia," came a soft voice from his right, "but please, you must tell my aunt all that you know and all that has occurred. I can assure you that she and I will listen closely and will not make any immediate conclusions."

He looked over at Miss Newton, seeing the gentle smile on her face and finding that even he let out a breath of relief at her words. Miss Newton's gaze flicked to his for a moment, her smile spreading just a little more before she looked away with warmth racing through her cheeks.

"My brother is right when he states that I have been accused of theft," Olivia began, making William almost sag with relief where he sat. "There have been four or five different incidents, but due to two gentlemen's testimony – both which have come at different times, society believes that I am the culprit."

William saw Lady Landerbelt frown, her eyes narrowing just a little. "Two gentlemen claim to have seen you stealing the jewels?"

"On two separate occasions, yes," Olivia replied, her shoulders slumping. "I did not do so, of course, and I cannot think why they would say that they saw me taking the jewels!"

There was a short silence. William dared not glance over at Miss Newton for fear that he would find her expression to be one of disbelief, given that her aunt appeared to be thinking everything over with a great deal of consideration.

"These gentlemen, Lady Olivia," Miss Newton said, quietly. "Who were they? Are you known to them?"

William shook his head, aware that his sister's eyes were filling with tears. "My sister does not know them at all, Miss

Newton. Lord Dewford and Lord Winchester, to be exact. Both viscounts, but neither of them having ever been introduced to Olivia nor myself."

"Which, unfortunately, makes their testimony carry a little more weight," Lady Landerbelt added slowly. "They have no motive for accusing you falsely, Lady Olivia, and therefore society will be inclined to believe them."

William clenched his fists as Olivia sniffed, pulling out her lace handkerchief.

"But they said they saw you with the jewels?" Miss Newton persisted, sitting forward in her seat. "Is that true? Did you handle any of the pieces that have been stolen?"

Olivia looked up and appeared miserable. "No, I did not. However, on the first occasion, at Lady Edgeware's ball, I was taking a few moments of rest in a quiet room a little away from the ballroom, and when I came out, a gentleman I did not know passed me. I now know it was Lord Dewford."

Lady Landerbelt sipped her tea, her eyes studying Olivia carefully over the rim. "And the second occasion?" she asked, setting the cup back down. "Did the same thing occur?"

Knowing what was coming, William felt himself grow tense. This was the moment that Olivia had been dreading, a moment that would tell him exactly what Lady Landerbelt thought of his sister's guilt or innocence.

"The second occasion was at Lord and Lady Bradford's ball," Olivia began, her voice shaking. "I was asked to take a turn outside, given that the ballroom was so hot and stuffy, as they are inclined to be."

"Of course," Lady Landerbelt murmured, clearly under-standing. "And did you go?"

"I did," Olivia replied softly. "The gentleman I was with led me out to the gardens and, as we walked, I spotted something catching the light. When I lifted it, I discovered the jewels and, astonished, turned to ask the gentleman who was with me, Lord Darnley, what I ought to do with it, but he was gone."

A frown began to burrow its way into Lady Landerbelt's expression, and William slowly felt his heart sink down towards his toes. She would not believe Olivia, just as the rest of society did not. His poor sister would, once again, be left to stand accused before the *beau monde* with only himself to stay by her side.

"At that moment," Olivia continued, "Lord Winchester – although I did not know his name at the time — came towards me and snatched the pendant from my hand."

"It was a pendant you found?" Miss Newton interrupted. "A single piece on a chain?"

Olivia nodded, her face white. "It was encrusted with diamonds, I believe, although I did not get to see it particularly well. As I said, a gentleman approached and snatched it from me, declaring that I had stolen it and was trying to find a way to hide it on my person out in the gardens so that I could steal it without anyone noticing." She shook her head, her eyes lowering to the ground. "Of course, I did not steal it, but the gentleman was insistent. Despite my protestations, I was asked to leave, and since then, the *ton* has refused to believe anything I have to say. Lord Dewford told his story of seeing me in the passageway at Lady Edgeware's ball, and my fate was sealed. They have simply rejected me, believing me to be guilty of all the thefts that have taken place. They have not allowed me a moment to defend myself, have not listened to a single word I have to say. Instead, they have listened to Lord Dewford and Lord Winchester, and even Lord Darnley, who now states that he did not ever ask me to take a turn with him in the gardens!" Her voice grew louder, only for her shoulders to slump and her head to lower, her eyes on the ground. "I have nothing and no one save my brother, Lady Landerbelt. To everyone else, I am already guilty."

There was a long, tense silence. William wanted to wrap his arm around his sister's shoulders to comfort her but chose instead to simply sit on his hands and wait, unable to bring himself to look into Lady Landerbelt's eyes, too afraid of what he would see there. To everyone else in the *beau monde,* Olivia was guilty of crimes she had not committed, and it seemed only he refused to accept her supposed guilt. Lady Landerbelt had been his last hope, praying that the lady who herself had been accused of something terrible, only to prove herself to be entirely innocent, might have sympathy with Olivia, might be willing to not accept the testimony of two different gentlemen.

"Well, well," Lady Landerbelt murmured, sitting back in her chair with a look of surprise on her face. "And so the *ton* has now decided that you are responsible for these five thefts, is that right, Lady Olivia? I presume there is no proof that you did so, however."

"They do not need any proof," William interjected bitterly. "What Lord Winchester saw and then concluded is enough for them. They have subjected my sister to a lifetime of misery and ridicule, where no one will trust her, where no one will even go near her, given that they believe her to be a thief. Her name is being dragged through the mud, and there is no one who can help us. It is quite wrong, Lady Landerbelt, you *must,* at the very least, agree about that."

Lady Landerbelt's eyes flickered from Olivia to Miss Newton and then back to William again, her face expressionless as she considered. William did not know what to do or what to say, feeling his whole body begin to grow weary as he waited for Lady Landerbelt's decision.

"My niece and I were to discuss this matter in private before

I made any kind of decision, but I can see from her expression what she already thinks," Lady Landerbelt murmured, a small smile tugging at the corners of her mouth. "It is all very strange, is it not, Lady Olivia? Why should you bear the blame for five separate incidents, when there is only one incident that should draw any kind of attention and can easily be explained away?"

William, feeling a spark of hope grow in his chest, looked over at his sister, who was staring blankly at Lady Landerbelt, clearly troubled by what the lady would say next.

"It is, of course, the rule that a gentleman's testimony always carries more weight than that of a lady," Lady Landerbelt continued with a slightly wry smile, "but that does not explain why two gentlemen who have never known you or been introduced to you, should be so quick to throw the blame at your feet."

Drawing in a long breath to steady his nerves, William looked back at Lady Landerbelt with hope now burning fiercely in his heart. "Does this mean, Lady Landerbelt, that you consider my sister to be innocent of what she has been accused of?"

Lady Landerbelt frowned, her lips pressing together for a moment. "Have you had your house open for a search to take place?" she asked, turning towards him. "I know it is always a scandal to have the constabulary in one's home, but under the circumstances, it is perhaps wise."

Olivia began to cry, tears falling down her cheeks like rain. "They have already been to my brother's townhouse, Lady Landerbelt," she whispered, as Miss Newton got to her feet and came to sit by Olivia's side. "It was more than a mortification to see them looking in every nook and cranny, and you should have seen the look on the staff's faces as they watched me allow the constabulary into my bedchamber. It was shameful indeed!"

"And, of course, they found nothing but Olivia's own jewelry," William added, glad that Miss Newton had shown such compassion towards his sister. "There was no sign of any of the supposed thefts in my home."

Lady Landerbelt nodded slowly, her eyes drifting back towards Olivia. "But that, of course, would not be enough to satisfy the *ton*, I suppose?"

William shook his head, lowering his gaze to the floor as a rush of anger tore through him. "No, indeed, Lady Landerbelt. They did not care one jot. I believe the rumors are now that my sister has somehow found a hiding place for them within the house itself, since most of the *beau monde* believe the constabulary to be less than thorough."

"That is unfortunate," Lady Landerbelt murmured, now looking a little more sympathetic. "And I can understand your upset, Lady Olivia. To be so accused and to have no one other than your brother to believe you to be innocent of the crime is something that I myself have endured." She smiled at Olivia, who drew in a long shuddering breath. "Do not fear. I am sure that myself and my niece will be able to help you."

William did not know what to say, feeling as though he was somehow fastened to his chair. Staring at Lady Landerbelt, he heard Olivia break down into tears once more, clearly overcome with relief that she was not to be turned away by Lady Landerbelt. Miss Newton was murmuring words of encouragement into Olivia's ear, whilst looking towards him with warmth in her emerald eyes.

A warmth that thrust William's heart back to life again, forcing it to beat all the quicker as he rose to his feet, bowing deeply towards Lady Landerbelt.

"I cannot thank you enough, Lady Landerbelt," he said, his hands curling into fists as he attempted to keep a hold of his composure. "You do not know what this means to us both."

"I can guess," Lady Landerbelt replied, with a small smile.

"But I appreciate your thanks. Now, Olivia – for we must get rid of all formality if we are to work with one another – you will have to go through this all again, in as much detail as you can manage, and I will take notes. Shall we do that tomorrow afternoon? Yes? Very good. Then, in two days' time, you shall accompany us to Lord and Lady Derbyshire's ball – and you too, of course, Lord Caversham. Do not fear; they will not refuse to have you attend, for Lady Derbyshire is a very dear friend of mine and will be quite sympathetic to your plight once I have explained it to her." She smiled as William retook his seat, feeling himself weak with relief and joy.

"And, of course, you must stay for dinner," Miss Newton added, as Lady Landerbelt smiled and nodded. "After all, what Lady Olivia has to say might take some time, and I am sure we will all be quite famished thereafter."

Lady Landerbelt chuckled. "Indeed, a very good idea, Catherine." She turned towards William, who was still feeling rather overwhelmed, smiling at him gently.

"Now, Lord Caversham, whilst I am talking to your sister tomorrow afternoon, might I leave Miss Newton in your charge? I know that she is very keen to discover the beauty of Hyde Park and I thought that—"

"Of course," William said at once, not realizing he had interrupted Lady Landerbelt such was his eagerness to agree. "I would be delighted."

Miss Newton, however, looked a little surprised, only to smile as he looked over at her, clearly a little taken aback that her aunt had suggested such a thing but accepting it regardless.

"Then it is settled," Lady Landerbelt said with a broad smile. "You shall return tomorrow afternoon, Olivia, and we will go through everything. Meanwhile, my niece shall go out walking with Lord Caversham and will, I hope, do what she is *supposed* to be doing and begin to enjoy her season here in London!"

Miss Newton laughed, bringing a smile to William's face. "I am sure that Lord Caversham and I will have a great deal to talk about, Aunt," she said and chuckled, as Lady Landerbelt smiled back at her. "And none of it will be to do with the thefts, of course."

"Of course," William repeated, smiling broadly back at Miss Newton, feeling as though the sun had just appeared from behind a cloud and was shining its loveliness onto him. "Thank you, Miss Newton. And our thanks to you, Lady Landerbelt. This is more than either of us ever hoped for."

He saw Olivia murmur something to Miss Newton, something which made Olivia press Miss Newton's arm and smile, the first smile he had seen in some time. There was, finally, a little bit of hope in his sister's mind, and William could not have been more grateful for that.

"Until tomorrow, then," Lady Landerbelt said, as the butler opened the door. "Thank you for coming, Lady Olivia, Lord Caversham. I am sure that, together, we will get to the bottom of this terrible matter." She grasped Olivia's hand, smiling down at her. "I am sure that you will be back out in society again very soon, Olivia, and the *ton* will be at your feet, such will be their disgrace."

There was a glimmer of anger in Lady Landerbelt's expression; something William had not expected but, as Olivia turned back towards him, he saw the same look in her eye also. Apparently, Lady Landerbelt and Miss Newton had managed to spark a flame in his sister's heart, making her suddenly determined to find a way to prove to the *ton* that she was not a thief. It brought him a great deal of delight to see her so changed, no longer the timid little mouse that was sure Lady Landerbelt would reject her almost outright.

"Until tomorrow, Lady Landerbelt," Olivia said gratefully. "And thank you. Thank you so very much."

"It will be our pleasure to help you," Miss Newton said, as they walked from the drawing room and into the foyer where the butler handed them their coat and gloves. "Good day, Lady Olivia. Good day, Lord Caversham. I look forward to seeing you again tomorrow."

atherine walked alongside Lord Caversham on their way
to stroll in Hyde Park with her maid trailing a few steps
behind them, thinking to herself that he was a very handsome
gentleman indeed, even though lines of worry had begun to fix
themselves to his brow. It was clear he was deeply worried for
his sister and her reputation, which she could well understand,
given that she had felt much the same way for her own aunt
when she had been accused of murder.

"I cannot tell you how glad I am that your aunt has been
willing to take such consideration over my sister," Lord Caversham murmured, as they walked. "And that you would listen to
her too, of course. It means a very great deal to me."

"You are very welcome, Lord Caversham," Catherine replied
with a smile. "It must have been difficult for you to approach my
aunt, however."

"Difficult?" He lifted one eyebrow and looked at her. "Why
do you say that?"

"Is not a gentleman's testimony not often considered to be
held in a higher regard than any lady's testimony?" she asked,
feeling herself bristle at the notion. "That was why my aunt had

to work so hard to prove that she was not, in fact, the person responsible for the death of her husband. She simply was considered unable to have any kind of clout and, initially, the constabulary refused to even speak to her when she indicated that she was able to prove her innocence." Taking a deep breath, Catherine tried her best not to become angry simply because she was recounting the series of events. "The men at the constabulary did not think her intelligent enough for them to even listen to, despite her status. They thought she would have some kind of half-witted idea as to why she could not possibly have done it, and it was only my father's wrath that forced them to change their minds."

Lord Caversham stopped suddenly, making Catherine stumble to a stop beside him, a little confused.

"My dear Miss Newton, I pray that you do not think me a gentleman of the same ilk as those in the constabulary," he exclaimed, looking a little insulted. "I have never once considered Lady Landerbelt to be a lady lacking intelligence, nor have I ever thought of myself better than she. Indeed, the reason I turned to her was because I myself was completely at a loss as to how to help my sister and, from what I knew of her, your aunt would have the competence that I lacked."

Catherine felt a rush of shame creep up into her face and neck, aware that her cheeks were beginning to burn with heat.

"I do apologize, Lord Caversham, if I insulted you in any way," she stammered, feeling completely at a loss as to what to say. "You are quite right to state that I ought not to put you in the same camp as the constabulary, especially given my limited experience with gentlemen of the gentry."

He nodded, his lips flattening as he regarded her, only for him to let out a long breath and turn away, shaking his head.

"But then perhaps that is to be expected, since you saw the ridicule Lady Landerbelt endured, when she was trying her best to declare her innocence," he murmured, beginning to walk along the pavement again. "I fear that I have not made a particularly good impression, Miss Newton."

"Nor I," she exclaimed, with a slightly rueful laugh. "My goodness, Lord Caversham, we are quite a pair are we not?"

He laughed, and the last of her tension drained away. "Indeed we are, Miss Newton, and I will admit that we have found ourselves in rather strange circumstances also for our first meeting and introduction!"

"I would say so," Catherine agreed, looking up at him and finding that his dark brown eyes were now warm instead of angry. "Although I am glad to see a gentleman take such concern over his sister. I have witnessed my father behave in the very same way towards my aunt when she found herself in difficulty, but from what I understand, that is often very rare. Gentlemen who are titled and with families of their own can, I think, be caught up in their own lives and forget about their sisters, particularly if they are not married and a burden on their finances."

"I would never consider Olivia a burden," came the fervent reply. "Although I will agree with what you have said regardless. I was blessed with a very dedicated father, who did not send me to Eton the moment I turned seven years of age. He ensured that our family was a happy one, and myself and Olivia formed a strong bond from a young age. I am grateful to him for that."

Catherine smiled up at him, finding her heart quickening just a little as he smiled back at her, feeling as though she had known the gentleman for a long time, instead of only a few hours. "You are a kind man, I think, Lord Caversham. That says a great deal about your character."

He looked away, clearly a little embarrassed at the compliment. "Thank you, Miss Newton. You are very good to say."

As they walked into Hyde Park, Catherine found her breath catching in her throat at the sheer size of it, suddenly overwhelmed by the great many carriages that were making their way about the place. The park seemed to be filled with the gentry, with gentleman and ladies milling about from here to there, whilst some sat on blankets seemingly enjoying a picnic.

"We do not have to stay for long, if you do not wish to," Lord Caversham murmured, evidently seeing her surprise. "The fashionable hour is always rather busy although, for myself, I much prefer it when it is quiet. I like to be able to hear the birds sing."

Tilting her head, Catherine regarded Lord Caversham with a small measure of surprise, thinking to herself that he was not the kind of gentleman she had expected. She had thought that those in the *ton* would delight greatly in spending the majority of their time being seen by others in the *beau monde* and would enjoy nothing but company and wonderful parties.

Apparently, Lord Caversham was not that kind of gentleman, and that warmed her heart.

"I can introduce you to some, if you wish it," he continued, evidently unaware of her scrutiny, "although I will say that they may not be all that favorable towards me, given that my sister is the one supposedly known to be a thief." Sighing heavily, he glanced at her with a sad smile on his lips. "Because I defend her and do not shout from the rooftops that she is, in fact, guilty of such a crime, I am looked down on by the rest of the *beau monde.* They cry scandal where there is none." He paused again, looking at her steadily. "In fact, Miss Newton, you may be tarred by merely being seen with me. I do apologize. I ought to have thought of this much sooner."

Wishing to calm him, Catherine settled one hand on his arm, which made him start in surprise. He looked at her in astonishment, the words dying on his lips as she smiled at him gently, feeling a mixture of compassion and anticipation.

"Lord Caversham, you forget that I have entered into this with my aunt willingly. I wish to be of aid to your sister and also to you. I think it greatly unfair that you have been treated so by the *beau monde,* and I find that it disinclines me towards anyone who would be so cruel towards you."

She saw him swallow, glancing down to where her hand rested gently on his arm before looking back up towards her face. Clearly, he was a little surprised by what she was doing but, despite that, Catherine felt herself grow all the more determined. It was deeply unfair of the *ton* to treat Lord Caversham and his sister in such an unfair manner and, whether it would stain her reputation or not, she was determined to be seen out with him.

"Now," she said, letting go of his arm and setting her bonnet a little straighter. "Shall we go into the fray, Lord Caversham? You may introduce me to anyone you please, for I trust your judgment entirely."

"That is very good of you to say, Miss Newton," he murmured, still standing completely still and looking at her as though she had lost her mind. "But are you quite sure?"

"I am more than sure, Lord Caversham," she interrupted firmly. "Now, might you offer me your arm? I worry that I may feel a little weary on our walk around the park and would be glad of your support."

Part of her wanted to laugh as Lord Caversham stared at her for a moment, his mouth a little ajar, before he gave himself a slight shake and did as she had asked, standing tall and offering her the support of his arm, which she took at once in her gloved hand. Heat rippled up her hand into her frame, a smile spreading across her face as they walked together into Hyde Park.

Right away, Catherine could feel a great many eyes on her as they walked together, although she could not say whether it was due to the fact that it was Lord Caversham walking in the park, or because they were interested in whom she might be. It did not take long, however, for a gentleman to approach them as they walked on their way, stopping directly in their path so that they had no other course but to stop.

"Lord Benston," Lord Caversham murmured, inclining his head. "You are taking the air today?"

"I am," Lord Benston grinned, with a smile that Catherine did not like. The man was tall and thin, with blue eyes that glittered almost malevolently as they passed over Catherine. "But I was forced to pause in my walk when I saw the most beautiful creature on your arm, Lord Caversham, and I felt sure that I had to rescue her from your clutches."

Lord Caversham tensed but said nothing, whilst Catherine herself felt herself bristle.

"Viscount Benston, my lady," the man continued, bowing gracefully towards Catherine. "And you must not be aware of whom you are walking with, my lady, for were you to know the truth about this gentleman, then I am sure—"

"I am more than aware, I thank you," Catherine interrupted firmly, lifting her chin a notch. "I am Miss Catherine Newton, Lord Benston. Daughter to Viscount Higgs and niece to Lady Landerbelt."

An awareness of the name jumped into Lord Benston's expression, and he grinned at her as though he had not just insulted Lord Caversham right in front of her.

"I see," he said, stepping a little closer. "How interesting. You must have a great many stories to tell about all that went on, I am sure."

Catherine lifted one eyebrow, hoping she looked a little disdainful. "I am not in the habit of gossiping about my aunt, Lord Benston," she replied coolly. "Nor do I find it agreeable that any gentleman or lady of the *ton* would wish to hear such things from me."

That took a little of the spark out of Lord Benston's eyes, for he looked away, clearing his throat as he did so.

"Regardless, Miss Newton, I would be delighted to introduce you to a few of my companions," Lord Benston continued, after a moment to gather his composure. "You see just over there? There are five gentlemen and a few young ladies I am sure would be delighted to make your acquaintance. Lord Dewford, Lord Dalrymple, Lord Higglesworth, Lord Winchester, and Lord Smithson. All of the highest caliber and just right to be introduced to a lady such as yourself. After all, it will mean that you will not lack for dance partners come the next ball."

Lord Caversham's arm grew taut under Catherine's hand and, despite the disgust over Lord Benston's treatment of Lord Caversham, Catherine knew that she could not allow this opportunity it pass her by. After all, she had recognized two of the names of the gentlemen who had been mentioned by Lord Benston.

"I only have a few minutes," she said quietly, pulling her hand from Lord Caversham and praying he understood. "Thank you, Lord Benston."

Lord Caversham narrowed his eyes as Lord Benston grinned, almost cackling as Catherine came to stand by him.

"Lord Caversham, might you wait for me?" Catherine continued, looking at him steadily and praying that he might meet her gaze instead of growling at Lord Benston. "I think, since I am new to society, that I *must* meet as many new acquaintances as I can, do you not think so?"

Finally, Lord Caversham looked in her direction, and with a jerky nod, let his brown eyes rest on her own green ones. Seeing the understanding there, Catherine let out a small, quiet sigh of relief and turned to Lord Benston, steeling herself as he offered her his arm.

"I think not, Lord Benston," she said calmly, beginning to

walk in the direction he had indicated. "After all, we are just introduced!" Leaving Lord Benston spluttering behind her, she continued to walk towards the group of gentlemen and ladies who were gathered around a park bench, praying that she would not have to spend too much time in what she guessed might be rather undesirable company.

4

O ne week later and William found himself growing rather fond of Miss Newton's company. They had been together almost every evening over the last sennight, and he had come to find her pleasant and rather agreeable company. Whilst Olivia and Lady Landerbelt talked in depth about what had occurred – as well as other subjects too, of course, he had spent the majority of his time with Miss Newton. She had brought back such light to his life that, at times, he wanted to express it to her but found that he was entirely lost for words. He began to look forward to their time together, especially when he was able to walk with her either in the park or towards a bookshop, albeit with a maid trailing behind them.

He had been rather disappointed when she had turned from him and gone to speak to Lord Winchester and the like but had realized that she had done so only because she'd thought it best for Olivia's sake. He'd been forced to seat himself on a bench some distance away, although he'd been sure to keep watch on her, as though afraid that one of the gentlemen might do something entirely untoward – which was a ridiculous thought since they were in the very public place of Hyde Park.

At the time, he'd struggled to understand why Miss Newton was laughing and talking so brightly with the men they'd only just told her had been the ones to lay blame at Olivia's feet, but when she'd approached him again, she'd explained at once what she'd been doing. To get to know Lord Winchester and Lord Dewford was, of course, to be seen as a good thing. That way, she might be able to continue her acquaintance with them, just in case they said anything about Olivia that might be of aid to them all. It had made sense the moment she'd explained it all, and he'd nodded gratefully, offering her his arm which she'd taken at once. That had made him almost glow with happiness, and he had managed to ignore the callous stares of the other gentlemen as they'd walked away.

Now, he found himself in one of London's bookshops. Each shelf was lined with beautifully bound books, yet he could not keep his mind from wandering to Miss Newton. There was not a book in the shop that could compare to the beauty of Miss Newton.

"My goodness, Lord Caversham, you look very pleased with yourself, I must say."

Glancing up in surprise, William realized too late that he'd been lost in his own thoughts whilst Miss Newton had been browsing the shelves for a new novel.

"Have you found a book that you particularly wish to purchase?" she asked, with one arched eyebrow. "Or were you thinking of something completely different?"

A flush crept up his spine, and William could only pray that it did not go into his cheeks. Clearing his throat a little gruffly, he gave a slight shrug. "I was merely dwelling on some particular thoughts, Miss Newton."

"Oh?" She shot him a small, lopsided smile, and William felt his heart quicken a little more. "Anything worth sharing?"

He could not exactly tell her that he had been dwelling on

thoughts of her now, could he? But yet, the urge to do precisely that grew within him.

"No," he managed to say, despite the urge to say the precise opposite. "No, not as yet."

She leaned against the bookshelf just a little, her eyes warm as she looked back at him with just a little more curiosity. "Then later, mayhap?"

Swallowing hard, William nodded and looked away, suddenly struck by Miss Newton's nearness. There was a softness to her, a delicacy that he had not expected to be so touched by. There was something in the way she was looking at him that made his heart quicken all the more and made his lungs feel fit to burst – but he dared not move. What was this urge that raced through him, that longed to know just how soft her skin might be if he should twine her fingers with his? What was this desire to have her close to him, to look down at her rosebud lips and...?

Suddenly, there was a tinkling of the bell above the bookshop door, and he heard the shopkeeper greet whoever entered, which interrupted his thoughts. As the fall of footsteps approached them, Lord Caversham knew that his reverie was about to end for the moment. And end it did, as the sound of a harsh, unwelcome voice filled the bookshop, making William wince. "Miss Newton?"

It was none other than Lord Dewford, and most likely there would be Lord Winchester and more of his friends just behind him.

"Oh dear," Miss Newton murmured, her eyes now drifting over his left shoulder. "Do excuse me for a moment, Lord Caversham. I had best deal with this rather quickly. Would you mind if we left quite soon?"

He held out his hand. "If you would but permit me, Miss Newton, I will purchase your books and make ready to leave."

She smiled at him, handing him the books, and for a

moment, it was as though it were just the two of them in the shop, standing together.

The air sparked between them, and Miss Newton seemed to glow with a radiant light as she smiled back at him. William's heart thundered wildly, his blood roaring in his ears – and then she was gone.

Making his way towards the front of the shop, William purchased the books and waited patiently for the shopkeeper to wrap them in brown paper and tie them with a ribbon. His eyes drifted to where Miss Newton and Lord Dewford were talking quietly, and he became aware that there was now not a single smile on Miss Newton's features. She clearly was not enjoying her conversation with Lord Dewford, and *that* brought William a thrill of delight.

Then, Miss Newton and Lord Dewford turned as one to face him, and William was struck by the sheer repugnance on Lord Dewford's face. It was clear that he disliked William intently, but as for the reason, William could not say. It could not simply be because Olivia was his sister, surely? That was no reason at all to be so disinclined towards a gentleman, and yet that curl of Lord Dewford's lip and the glare in his eyes said the opposite entirely.

"I think we had best go now," Miss Newton said hurriedly, as the shopkeeper handed William the books. "You have no partic-ular urge to remain, do you?"

She looked up at him with anxiety in her eyes, and William shook his head. Letting out a sigh of relief, Miss Newton gave him a tight smile.

"Good, I am glad to hear it. Lord Dewford has been so kind as to inform me that Lord Winchester and one or two more particular friends of his are on their way to this very shop, although I do not think they intend to so much as step inside! Lord Dewford is a little early, which is why he came inside."

William frowned. "Then why are they coming here?"

She shook her head, a thin line forming her lips. "They are doing as all gentlemen do, Lord Caversham. They intend to parade themselves through town and then go on to Hyde Park for the fashionable hour."

He could see that this idea displeased her very much and could not help but feel a distinct solidarity with her. "I quite agree that such a thing is ridiculous, Miss Newton. Come now, we should make our way back."

Holding the door for her, he waited until she had made her way past him before coming outside himself and offered her his arm immediately. It was a habit they had begun the very day they had first gone out walking together, and William was glad that she always so eagerly accepted.

"You do not care much for being seen by society, I think, Lord Caversham," Miss Newton began, as they walked back to Lady Landerbelt's townhouse. "You are not inclined to parade around Hyde Park at the fashionable hour, are you?"

He gave a small, rueful shrug. "That is perhaps because I am not exactly favorable with the *ton,* Miss Newton."

Her eyes brightened as she smiled into his eyes. "No, indeed, that is not it at all. Even before all this happened, I do not think that you were eager to be seen by the *beau monde*, nor would I say that about Lady Olivia either!"

Chuckling, he patted her hand without thinking and looked down at her, realizing that they were walking rather slowly.

"Indeed, Miss Newton, you know us both very well already," he murmured, the smile fading from his face as he was caught by the intensity in her eyes. "We both do not care for society's ways, although we do both enjoy balls and the like. I look forward to the honor of dancing with you next week at the ball. How your aunt has managed to procure invitations for myself and Olivia, I cannot understand, although I am profoundly grateful!"

Now, it was Miss Newton's turn to chuckle. "My aunt has a great many connections and a good deal of influence, Lord Caversham. The fact that she was once accused of murder has a great many tongues wagging, and it is almost a blessing to any member of the *ton* to have her present at their social occasion." She gave a small shrug, although her smile remained. "She is a wonderful lady, and I have much to learn from her."

The compliment came to his lips before he could stop it. "You are wonderful in your own right, Miss Newton."

She glanced up at him sharply, although her lips curved gently.

"I know this is most presumptuous, but might I ask you to consider allowing my court, Miss Newton?"

William was astonished that such a question had come to his lips and, not only that, but that he had spoken it aloud. He had not meant to say anything of the sort, and yet now the words could not be taken back. His heart was beating so loudly, he was quite sure Miss Newton would be able to hear it, and his mouth had gone so dry that it was as if sand had filled his throat.

Miss Newton, however, did not appear to be astonished in any way. Instead, her gentle smile warmed his heart, her hand tightening on his arm just a little.

"I would be glad to accept the offer of your courtship, Lord Caversham," she began, "but do you not think it might be best to wait until this mess with Lady Olivia is done with? Once her name is cleared – for I am sure my aunt will be able to do so – then we might be free to continue on just as we please, without anything to trouble us. Besides which, I do not want Lady Olivia to think that we have forgotten about her rather difficult situation in place of our own thoughts and our own happiness!"

Finding himself nodding, William tried to sort out his scrambled thoughts, aware that he was making something of a cake of himself and yet finding that he did not know what else to do.

"You do not mind, Lord Caversham?" Miss Newton's eyes were anxious now, peering up into his as he struggled to answer.

Shaking his head, William tried to clear his throat before he spoke. "Indeed, Miss Newton, I am simply overcome with happiness. I shall wait for as long as necessary, of course. You are quite right. Thank you, Miss Newton for your dear consideration of my sister." Frustrated that he had not done so himself, he turned his head and looked directly along the pavement, trying not to allow his embarrassment to show in his features.

Laughing gently, Miss Newton shook her head. "You need not criticize yourself, Lord Caversham, for you are as good a brother as anyone could ask for, I am certain. It will all be sorted out very soon, I am sure, and then you will be able to put your question as regards our courtship to my aunt, for she will want to be asked first. She will not refuse you, however, of that, I know." Her emerald eyes seemed to glitter with nothing more than delight and happiness, as she looked up at him, and William felt a deep sigh of both relief and joy release from deep within him.

"I am very glad to hear it, Miss Newton," he murmured, as they approached Lady Landerbelt's townhouse. "I must say I do not think I have been this content in some time." He looked down at her fondly, feeling his heart swell with affection in his chest. "And I have you to thank for that, Miss Newton."

There came no response from the lady, although a beautiful smile spread across her face and her green eyes sparkled with joy. A smile that became fixed in William's memory, as they made their way up the stone steps and back into Lady Landerbelt's home.

5

"How awful!"

Miss Catherine Newton looked up at Lord Winchester's arrogant face and forced herself to keep her expression astonished, even though she was recoiling within herself. After having been introduced to the gentleman a little over a week ago, she now found herself dancing with him at Lord and Lady Allen's ball, even though she had no desire to be anywhere near the gentleman. Lord Winchester was just as she had expected: proud, haughty, and filled with such a sense of self-importance that it was all Catherine could do to keep her expression sweet.

She disliked the man intently.

However, her aunt had declared the idea to be a marvelous one, encouraging Catherine to continue with her association with both Lord Winchester and Lord Dewford in the hopes that Catherine might be able to uncover something that would help them clear Olivia's name.

"Indeed, it is truly the worst thing that I have ever witnessed," Lord Winchester declared, as they came back together again. "To see a lady of quality take the pendant so brazenly quite seared my mind. I am afraid I might never forget it."

Catherine allowed herself a small frown as she curtsied, filled with relief that their dance was now over. "I am quite sure that the lady herself, however, said that she did not take the pendant but that, rather, she simply found the pendant."

Lord Winchester guffawed and offered her his arm as they walked from the dance floor. "I hardly think that to be the case, Miss Newton, do you? A guilty excuse, mayhap, but nothing more than that."

"Still," Catherine mused aloud, her eyes alighting on her aunt, who was now standing by Olivia's side, "one must question why she would do such a thing when I know her brother has more than enough wealth to care for her."

Shaking his head, Lord Winchester let out a long, heavy sigh as though he were sorry for her, sorry that she could believe such a thing. "My dear Miss Newton, you are much too good to hear such terrible things, I am quite sure. Whilst you are quite right to say that Lord Caversham has more than enough wealth, he is a selfish gentleman by all accounts and, even more so, it has been said that he told his sister he would not give her a penny more if she was not wed by the end of this Season! Of course, Lady Olivia is handsome enough for most gentlemen, were it not for that shy demeanor of hers, which makes her appear like a church mouse!"

Feeling her anger growing steadily, Catherine let her fingers curl tightly, aware that they nearly cut into the soft skin of her gloved palms but yet unable to do anything else. She did not like how Lord Winchester could speak so unfavorably about Lady Olivia and Lord Caversham, particularly when she was not yet particularly well acquainted with him, but the gentleman did not want to hold anything back, it seemed. He was rather proud of himself, as though shaming Lady Olivia was his life's greatest achievement, even though Catherine knew it was simply his word against Lady Olivia's.

And yet, that was the way the world worked. A gentleman's testimony was given a great deal more weight than a lady's.

"It is all very unfair," she muttered aloud, only for Lord Winchester to look down at her in puzzlement.

She gave a small smile, aware that her face was now blossoming with heat. "For Lord Caversham to treat his sister so," she explained, seeing Lord Winchester nod and immediately feeling a thrill of relief. "Terrible, is it not?"

"Indeed," Lord Winchester replied, with such a degree of sadness that Catherine would have been quite taken in, had she not been so repelled by Lord Winchester's character. "The poor creature must have tried to steal those jewels so that she would be set up for life, should the worst happen."

"Jewels?" Catherine repeated, in an attempt to look confused. "There was more than one incident?"

Lord Winchester nodded, releasing her arm as they moved back into the crowd of guests. "My dear friend, Lord Dewford, witnessed the other theft, which came before my own incident," he explained, his eyes landing on hers with such an intensity that Catherine was forced to draw in a breath. "I am sure he would be glad to explain it all to you and your aunt, given that it appears she is so enamored with the lady."

Glancing over her shoulder, Catherine saw with satisfaction that her aunt was busy talking with two particular gentlemen, whilst Olivia remained by her side.

"Yes, indeed," she murmured, looking back towards Lord Winchester with an appearance of gratitude. "Might you and Lord Dewford be willing to come to tea, perhaps tomorrow? Or in two days hence?"

Lord Winchester grinned, his eyes roving over her for a moment, which left Catherine feeling more than a little uncomfortable. "That would be wonderful," he murmured, bowing his head. "Thank you, Miss Newton."

"Thank you for all you have shared with me, Lord Winchester," Catherine replied, praying that she sounded truly grateful. "I will share such things with my aunt, of course."

"And you must make sure not to dance with Lord Caversham," Lord Winchester warned firmly. "It is not the done thing."

Catherine sighed dramatically, casting her eyes up to the ceiling. "Alas, if only you had told me such a thing before now, Lord Winchester! I have him down for two dances – one of which is the waltz – and I am afraid I have no other choice but to do so."

To her very great surprise, something like anger burned across Lord Winchester's expression, although it was gone in a moment. Catherine blinked, rather taken aback, only for Lord Winchester to bow over her hand, looking more than a little regretful.

"Then you will know not to allow him such a thing at the next ball you attend," he said, as Catherine felt her skin crawl from where he touched her fingers. Even though they both wore gloves, she could feel the heat of his hand on her skin and wanted to do nothing more than pull her hand away almost at once, hating that he was still so very near to her. "Good evening, Miss Newton. I do hope you enjoy the rest of the evening."

"Good evening, Lord Winchester," she murmured, bobbing a curtsy as he turned on his heel and left, leaving her with such a sense of relief that she immediately felt the urge to sit down.

Lord Winchester was not a pleasant gentleman, she was sure of that, but his arrogance and confidence told her that he would make almost any member of the *ton* willing to listen and believe whatever he said. Not her, of course, since she had such a dislike for him given how he treated Lord Caversham and how poorly he spoke of Lady Olivia, but to put on such a pretense had been more than a little difficult.

She would have to tell her aunt that Lord Winchester and Lord Dewford were coming for afternoon tea in two days' time – something she knew would please her aunt since she would be able to ask the gentlemen as many questions as she wished – and, of course, Catherine intended to be present also. As much as she did not care for Lord Winchester, she wanted to hear what he had to say for himself, praying that somehow, he would catch himself out and reveal something.

And yet, a sense of despondency settled over her. Lord Winchester was quite sure of himself, and she was certain that Lord Dewford would be much the same. What if they did not have anything particular to say? What if there was nothing Catherine or her aunt could catch them out on? Then they would be just as they were at this very moment, struggling to find a way to break the gentleman's testimony and free Lady Olivia from the rumors that bound her.

"You look troubled."

She started, turning around to see Lord Caversham standing just beside her, his eyes searching her face.

"Lord Winchester did not speak well of me, I presume."

She shook her head, wishing she could take his arm and press it in sympathy. "Nor of your sister, which angered me a very great deal."

A small shrug lifted his shoulders. "It is to be expected."

Catherine sighed heavily, her gaze drifting towards Lady Olivia, who was now blushing furiously as a gentleman signed her dance card, only for it then to be handed over to another gentleman, who did the same. Her heart lifted, her lips curving into a smile as she caught Lord Caversham's arm.

"Oh, look!" she breathed, forcing him to turn around. "Your sister has partners at long last!"

Lord Caversham chuckled. "You must thank your aunt for that, Miss Newton. She has done wonders this evening, not only in getting my sister into the ball in the first place!" He shook his head, his smile lingering in his eyes. "It seems that she has some gentlemen of her acquaintance who will do whatever she wishes, regardless of what has been said about my sister."

As one of the gentlemen turned away from Aunt Angelica and Lady Olivia, Catherine caught her breath, her hand going to her mouth. It was none other than Lord Thorndyke, who had been the late Lord Landerbelt's dearest friend. He had never taken to Lady Landerbelt and had remained thoroughly silent as the investigation into Lord Landerbelt's death had continued. Catherine had never liked him.

"Is something the matter, Miss Newton?"

Trying to shake her head in Lord Caversham's direction, Catherine found that she could not take her eyes from Lord Thorndyke, astonished to see him with something like a smile on his face as he walked away. She made a note to discuss the man's presence with her aunt whenever she could, for this was more than a little astonishing.

"I just saw someone that I had not expected to set eyes on in a very long time," she explained, dragging her eyes away from Lord Thorndyke and turning them back to Lord Caversham, who was still looking at her with concern. "But I will say that I had a rather interesting conversation with Lord Winchester, which I must discuss with you."

Lord Caversham nodded at once, looking more than a little eager. "It is, however, our dance, Miss Newton. Would you wish to take to the floor or might you prefer a quiet stroll around the room?"

She smiled at him, her heart glad that he understood her urgency when it came to talking over what Lord Winchester had shared.

"A walk would perhaps be more suitable," she agreed, as he offered his arm. "My aunt will not mind, I assure you."

He laughed, as he looked down her, a gentle fondness in his eyes. "Your aunt is unlike any other lady of my acquaintance, Miss Newton. I am sure she will, however, not take kindly to me taking you away somewhere quiet without her knowledge. Might we at least inform her of where we are to go? I would not like to disappoint her in any way."

With a small shrug, Catherine walked towards her aunt, who was now standing in a quiet corner of the ballroom, talking to Lady Olivia. She was almost glad that Lord Caversham had been so protective of her. There was a deepening of their acquaintance already, she could feel it. It still felt to her as though she had known Lord Caversham for a great deal longer than she had in actuality, although she could not be certain that he felt the same way.

"Aunt, I am to walk with Lord Caversham for a time," she said, flashing Lady Olivia a quick smile. "I danced with Lord Winchester, and there is something I must discuss with him."

Aunt Angelica nodded, although the smile fled from her face. "Of course. Nothing untoward, I hope?"

Catherine shook her head. "No, Aunt Angelica. However, what I will say is that I think Lord Winchester's reasons for laying such blame at Lady Olivia's feet is not to do with Lady Olivia herself but rather to do with Lord Caversham."

"Lord Caversham?" Aunt Angelica repeated, her eyes turning now to Lord Caversham, who stood next to Catherine with a look of confusion on his face. "And why is that?"

Half wishing she had not said a thing and had, instead, simply gone out to walk with Lord Caversham with her aunt's permission, Catherine bit back a sigh and explained what she had seen.

"There existed a great deal of anger on Lord Winchester's

face when I mentioned that I had no other option but to dance with you, Lord Caversham," she explained, turning towards him. "Have you any dealing with Lord Winchester? Is there some reason that he wants to shame your family and your title?"

She watched as Lord Caversham dropped his gaze, suddenly appearing rather uncomfortable. A stone settled in her stomach as she looked back at him steadily, remembering how he had denied ever being introduced to them. Was he, in fact, hiding the truth from them all?

"No, I have never had any dealings with Lord Winchester," Lord Caversham said, heavily, his gaze dropping. "Nor with Lord Dewford."

Still feeling as though he were holding something back, Catherine narrowed her gaze and studied him carefully. Her aunt, apparently feeling much the same way, cleared her throat.

"I have the distinct impression, Lord Caversham, that you have not been entirely truthful about something to do with Lord Winchester and Lord Dewford," she said quietly, aware of the guests milling around them all. "If there is something that you wish to tell us all, I suggest you do so now."

Lord Caversham's shoulders slumped as he sent a rather sad look towards Lady Olivia.

"Everything I have said is true," he said slowly. "One thing I did not mention, however, was that I once was called upon by another gentleman who claimed to be Lord Winchester's brother, as though that would make a difference to what I thought of him!"

Catherine frowned, rather confused. "What do you mean, Lord Caversham?"

Lord Caversham let out a long breath, his eyes still on Olivia. "Lord Winchester's younger brother, the honorable Henry Cartwright, appeared on my doorstep and proclaimed his love for Olivia, begging for her hand in marriage."

Catherine heard Olivia gasp and turned to see the young woman's eyes filling with tears as she gazed back at her brother, clearly distressed that he had never revealed such a thing to her before.

"Naturally, I refused him," Lord Caversham continued, without any sense of regret in his words. "The man was in my study, weaving back and forth with such liquor on his breath that I was surprised he could stand! He told me that he had been introduced to you, Olivia, and was desperately in love with you. I told him, in no uncertain terms that his dream of taking you as his wife would never come to fulfilment. I did not need to know anything more of his character, Olivia, for to see him so drunk and so eager to wed you after only one introduction, was more than I could stand! I knew he would not be a suitable husband for you, and so..." He sighed again, passing one hand over his eyes. "And so, I had him ejected from the house."

No one said a word for a few moments, tension beginning to coil in each one. Catherine could see that her aunt was somewhat frustrated that Lord Caversham had not said this before now, but in his defense, she could understand why he had chosen not to do so. He had not wanted Olivia to be even more embarrassed than she was already and had clearly never thought that such a thing had any bearing on the present situation.

"Why did you not say so before, Caversham?" Olivia's voice was soft, her words broken with emotion, as she came over to her brother, putting one hand on his arm.

"I did not want you to be troubled by it," he replied quietly. "You were already enjoying a wonderful Season, and I thought...."

"And now this Season, we have this matter of Lady Olivia's supposed guilt," Lady Landerbelt interjected, her brows furrowing. "I can see the progression from one to the next, Lord Caversham, even if you cannot."

Lord Caversham lifted his chin, his jaw working for a moment before he answered. "I did not think in the same way as you, Lady Landerbelt. I apologize for not bringing it to your attention before."

Lady Landerbelt nodded, as Catherine felt torn between sympathy for Lord Caversham's situation and irritation with him for not telling them this when they had first met.

"Where is the honorable William Cartwright now?" she asked, aware that Lord Caversham was no longer able to meet her gaze. "Might we speak with him about this?"

Lord Caversham shrugged, his head lowering. "I do not know, Miss Newton."

"Well," Lady Landerbelt said briskly. "At least this gives us something to go on, Lord Caversham. We shall find this Mr. Cartwright and deal with the matter from there."

6

Lady Angelica Landerbelt was forced to put on a bright smile as Lord Winchester and Lord Dewford entered her drawing room. She did not particularly want to be amiable towards them, nor did she want to hear whatever disparaging things they were certain to say about Lady Olivia, but she knew that this was the best way for her to discern what they thought about Lord Caversham. They might even accidentally let something slip, which might give her insight into their motives.

"How wonderful to meet you, Lord Winchester, Lord Dewford," she exclaimed, as Catherine made the introductions. "My niece has been very good in telling me all that she knows of you, and I must say I am troubled to hear that there may be some difficulties as regards my new friendship with Lady Olivia!"

She had startled them, she could see, but she did not want to waste any time on formality or other such trivial conversation. Going directly to the point, she sat down and gestured for the maids to bring in the trays for them all. As the maids set down trays filled with tea and pastries, it gave Lady Landerbelt a chance to observe the gentlemen, noticing that they appeared to be seemingly at ease.

"Miss Newton informs me that you warned her away from Lord Caversham, which was *most* good of you to do, Lord Winchester," she continued, as Catherine leaned forward to pour the tea. "She is new to society and, of course, as I am sure you know, I am only just returned to London myself after what has been a very trying time in my life."

Lord Winchester, his good looks and charm obvious from the moment he had stepped inside, nodded and smiled beatifically. "I had heard, Lady Landerbelt, and I am very glad indeed that you were cleared of all such horrific accusations."

She nodded, looking at him steadily. "To lose a husband and then be accused of having a hand in his death was a very painful experience, Lord Winchester. I miss my husband every day."

"I quite understand," he murmured, as something like grief flickered in his eyes. "To lose a family member is a very painful experience, especially if they are in the prime of life."

Angelica caught her breath, aware that Lord Winchester was now looking in the opposite direction, his shoulders slumped. The way he had spoken of the death of a loved one told her that he had experienced such a thing himself and, for a moment, she wondered if it was his brother that he was talking of – although it could easily have been his late father.

"Indeed," Lord Dewford added, drawing her attention back again. "A very painful trial, I am sure." He appeared to be surveying them both from under dark eyebrows, his expression much less open than Lord Winchester's. "It must have been a very difficult time for you, Lady Landerbelt."

She sighed dramatically, catching Catherine's eye and forcing her niece to hide a smile.

"It was truly terrible, which is why I am very concerned to hear that my association with Lady Olivia might in itself be a troubling one! I do not need to have any more scandal attached to my name, Lord Winchester. Might you tell me what it is you have such concerns about?"

There was a short pause as Lord Winchester and Lord Dewford shared a glance, as though wondering whether they ought to be honest with her or not. Lady Landerbelt gave them that moment to silently make their decision but then decided to give them a slight nudge of encouragement so that she and Catherine could perhaps garner additional information.

"I am sure that Miss Newton and I would be in your debt," she murmured, lifting her teacup to her lips and praying that Catherine would understand what she was trying to do.

Thankfully, her niece did.

"I am already very grateful to you, Lord Winchester, for what you told me at the ball," Catherine agreed, leaning forward and capturing Lord Winchester's attention with her bright, shining eyes. "You are truly a kind gentleman, I am sure of it."

Lord Winchester almost puffed out his chest with pride, whilst Lord Dewford looked a little less uneasy, his eyes captured by the smile on Catherine's face. It was just as well, Angelica thought, that her niece was rather pretty and came with a good dowry as well, for these two gentlemen were very easily captured by both.

"My dear Miss Newton, you need not thank me so efferves-cently," Lord Winchester said grandly. "I am only doing what I believe to be right. Lady Olivia is a thief—and all of society knows it."

Aware of the tension that wrapped itself around her heart at the mention of Olivia's name, Angelica felt herself grow stiff. She wanted to throw this gentleman from her house for saying such a thing but, knowing that she had to continue with her façade, forced herself to appear horrified.

"But why has she not been thrown from society?" she asked,

as Catherine shook her head, in apparent despair. "I would have thought...?"

"She claims that she did not do anything of the sort," Lord Dewford said, sighing. "However, Lord Winchester saw her with the pendant and, before that, I was sure she had taken another item from Lady Edgeware – a ruby necklace."

"My goodness," Angelica murmured, with what she hoped was a sorrowful expression on her face. "The lady, of course, claims to be innocent, I presume?"

"Of course!" Lord Winchester exclaimed, shaking his head. "In fact, Lord Bradford declared that he would not place the blame on Lady Olivia's shoulders when it came to the theft of the pendant, believing her story that she had simply found it in the grounds and picked it up." He shook his head, sniffing disparagingly. "Of course, Lord Bradford was always inclined to believe a pretty face, even if his own wife believes Lady Olivia to be the guilty one."

This was news to Angelica, who saw Catherine's eyebrows shoot towards her hair as she gazed at Lord Dewford, surprised that the gentleman to whom the pendant belonged did not, in fact, believe Olivia to be the thief.

"That explains why she was not reprimanded by the constabulary," Angelica murmured softly. "I do believe Lady Olivia told me herself that they had searched her brother's home with no sign of this ruby necklace anywhere."

Lord Winchester laughed a harsh, scornful laugh. "Of course they did not! Lady Olivia is as sly as they come and, given that she had some time between taking the necklace and the search of the townhouse, it is little wonder that the constabulary found nothing of note! It is quite clear that she has taken it somewhere else to hide it."

"And should someone find it, I suppose that might secure her guilt," Catherine added slowly. "Perhaps, then, I might keep up my acquaintance with Lord Caversham and Lady Olivia, Aunt?"

Angelica arched a brow as her niece turned towards her, aware of how brightly her eyes were shining. Clearly, her niece had an idea.

"Why would I let you do such a thing?" she asked sternly, hoping Catherine could see why she must act so horrified. "To be near to them would surely sully your own reputation, my dear!"

"Not if Lord Winchester and Lord Dewford know what I am about," Catherine replied quickly, sending Lord Winchester a warm smile. "They know that I will be attempting to find the ruby necklace in Lord Caversham's home, or at least be able to wrangle a clue from Lady Olivia's lips somehow."

There was a short silence and, much to Angelica's surprise, Lord Winchester was nodding with a slow smile spreading across his face as he looked back at Catherine.

The man was a fool.

"If you are set on the idea, then I am sure that society will be grateful to you for it, Miss Newton," he said, now ignoring Angelica completely. "I will, of course, ensure that your reputation is not sullied in any way, as will Lord Dewford, I am sure."

Lord Dewford dutifully nodded, his eyes flickering between Angelica and Catherine, as though he was not quite as sure as his friend.

"And, of course, you must continue to inform us about anything that you find," Lord Winchester continued, smiling broadly. "After all, I would be glad to spend more time in your company, Miss Newton."

Catherine smiled and ducked her head, although no rosy blush came to her cheeks as it might should she truly be over-whelmed by such a compliment. Angelica wanted to applaud her for such a performance, but instead cleared her throat and kept her lips thin.

"Gentlemen, you must see that I cannot so readily agree to this course of action," she exclaimed, shaking her head. "My niece is very precious indeed, and I cannot allow her reputation to be damaged in any way, not when she is meant to be seeking a good match for herself."

Lord Winchester turned his smile towards her, as did Lord Dewford.

"My dear lady, I will ensure that no harm comes to her reputation," he said, smoothly. "Should there be any questions about her association with either Lord Caversham or Lady Olivia, then I will be able to answer them in a way that will put your niece in the very best of lights."

She frowned. "And how will you do that, Lord Winchester?"

He chuckled, his expression warm. "I have ways and means, Lady Landerbelt. Being influential in society has its uses!"

Still not willing to appear to give in so easily, Angelica made a meal over sighing and shaking her head, forcing a few minutes of silence to pass before she agreed with Catherine's intentions.

"But I shall ensure to keep my acquaintance with the lady also," she said firmly, ignoring Lord Dewford's frown. "I must know what is being said, Catherine, and to do that I absolutely insist on being nearby. Do not argue with me on this, my dear niece." She held up one hand, and Catherine sighed heavily, giving a slightly rueful smile in Lord Winchester's direction.

"Lord Winchester, Lord Dewford, I am forever in your debt for explaining such things to me," Angelica continued, as the gentlemen smiled and nodded. "You have done both myself and my niece a very great service. I just hope that we might be able to repay such kindness in proving Lady Olivia's guilt."

Lord Winchester sighed, shaking his head. "I fear that you may not be able to do so, Lady Landerbelt, but regardless of that,

I am glad to be in your confidence and to continue my acquaintance with Miss Newton."

"As am I," Catherine said heartily. "Thank you again, Lord Winchester."

The gentlemen rose as one, bowing over Angelica's hand, although she caught Lord Winchester pressing a light kiss to the back of Catherine's hand, which made her niece squirm – but not from delight, she was sure of it. Moments later the butler appeared to escort the gentlemen out. The two women continued with their façade until the door to the drawing from closed firmly behind Lord Winchester and Lord Dewford, finally allowing them to collapse back in their chairs, the tension and strain finally gone.

"You did very well, my dear," Angelica said, applauding her niece. "I am sure Lord Caversham and Lady Olivia will be very pleased."

"I do hope they will not mind the pretense," Catherine replied, a little worried. "It is all to clear her name, of course, although I am not yet certain how we are to go about that."

Angelica grinned, her eyes dancing. "You are pretending to draw close to Lady Olivia, whilst ensuring that Lord Winchester and Lord Dewford are informed of your progress. You are not to look for clues from Lady Olivia, as you promised, but rather from Lord Winchester or Dewford instead."

"Which I will then pass on to you," Catherine continued slowly, understanding in her eyes.

Angelica nodded. "Lord Winchester clearly is quite taken with you, which is no surprise since you are the embodiment of grace and beauty, but you must use that to your advantage, no matter how disinclined you might be towards that idea." She laughed as Catherine grimaced, aware that she disliked Lord Winchester intensely.

"At least I can continue my acquaintance with Lord Caversham uninterrupted," Catherine murmured, almost to herself. "That is something I am most grateful for."

There was no astonishment in Angelica's response, for she had seen how her niece and Lord Caversham had taken to one another over the last few days and, finding the man to be more than agreeable, was more than happy to push her niece in that direction.

"I am sure he will be glad to hear of it also," she murmured, as Catherine blushed. "He is a good man, I think, Catherine."

"We are nothing more than acquaintances," Catherine replied hastily. "Although I confess that it does often feel as though we have been friends for a long time." She tilted her head, her eyes narrowing just a little as she looked back at Angelica. "And did I not see Lord Thorndyke with Lady Olivia at the ball two nights previous? I quite forgot to ask you about him."

A ripple of heat made its way up from Angelica's core, her skin prickling uncomfortably. "I was as surprised to see him as you," she managed to say, not wanting to go into too much detail about the Earl of Thorndyke, who had been her late husband's very dear friend.

"Why is he in town?" Catherine persisted, still looking rather curious. "Did he not say he would never come near you again? And yet, here he is?"

"Here he is," Angelica murmured, recalling how astonished she'd been to see him and how quickly she'd had to hide her surprise for the sake of Olivia. She had been even more astonished when he'd not only greeted her and Olivia cordially but had then sought to dance with Lady Olivia – although he had not asked her the same thing, of course. How well she could remember his furious face as he'd declared her guilty of murdering her husband, how he'd been the one to tell the constabulary that she was responsible.

And, of course, she remembered her pride as she'd stood in the room where her husband had been found dead, looking Lord Thorndyke directly in the eye as the constabulary had declared her innocent, telling Lord Thorndyke that Lord Landerbelt had, in fact, been killed by a recently spurned lover.

He'd gone sheet white at that, staring at her with a haunted look in his eyes, as though he'd never given even a single thought to the belief that she might, in fact, be innocent.

"Landerbelt had a mistress?" he had said with cold, bloodless lips. "Truly?"

She'd said nothing but had turned on her heel and walked from the room with her head held high. Even now, she could not quite understand it. Had he truly never considered that Landerbelt had mistresses, had lovers outside of the marriage bed, and that one of them might have been responsible?

"Are you to see him again?"

Drawn back to the present, Angelica shrugged, trying to set the troubling figure of Lord Thorndyke to one side. "I doubt it," she replied, as calmly as she could. "We have very little to say to one another."

"And he has never apologized?"

Angelica shook her head. "The man is too proud to ever say anything of the sort, Catherine. Besides, I do not require an apology from him. I was always sure of my innocence, even if he was not. Our paths need never cross again."

Catherine nodded slowly, still looking a little curious although nothing escaped her lips.

"Now, you must write a note to Lord Winchester at once, must you not?" Angelica asked a little more briskly, as she threw aside the topic of Lord Thorndyke. "Whilst I do think that it is important that Lord Caversham and Lady Olivia know of our plans, I think it might be best to wait until we have made a little more progress, even though I have a suspicion about Lord Winchester and his brother."

"Oh?"

Recalling how distraught Lord Winchester had appeared when he had talked of losing a family member, even though it had only been for a moment or two, Angelica gave her niece a small, sad smile. "Indeed. Aside from his arrogance and sheer wrongdoing, I am quite sure that Lord Winchester's brother is dead."

Catherine's eyes widened. "Dead?"

Growing more and more certain with every moment that passed, Angelica inclined her head. "I believe so. And that, my dear, might give us a motive for the supposed thefts."

Now frowning a little, Catherine pursed her lips together as she thought. "You believe that Lord Winchester has done all this as some sort of revenge? Even though Lady Olivia did not ever see his brother, and it was, in fact, Lord Caversham who refused him?"

Nodding slowly, Angelica caught the confusion in Catherine's eyes and smiled. "It will take a little more consideration and, perhaps, a little more information from Lord Winchester, but I am sure that, by the end of the Season, we will have the truth."

A slow smile began to spread across Catherine's face as she took in Angelica's expression. "I do hope so, Aunt Angelica. For Lady Olivia's sake."

7

W illiam walked into the ballroom with his sister on his arm, praying that no one would give Olivia the cut direct. She had been anxious enough about coming out this evening, and it was made even more difficult by the fact that it had been some days since they had last seen Lady Landerbelt and Miss Newton.

It was, of course, quite acceptable to be without their company for a short time, but even so, William had found himself growing almost listless as he struggled to turn his thoughts anywhere other than Miss Newton. Even Olivia had noticed and teased him mercilessly for an hour or so, until he had been forced to admit that, yes, he did find Miss Newton a very agreeable creature and was, in fact, missing her company.

However, whilst Olivia had smiled for an hour or so, she had soon fallen back into melancholy, which he had been unable to prevent himself from joining. She was worried that due to his lack of forthrightness about Lord Winchester's brother, Lady Landerbelt and Miss Newton might no longer wish to aid them. He had tried to encourage Olivia in this, of course, stating that she had nothing to concern herself with since she had not known about this gentleman either, whilst underneath it all, he felt just as anxious himself.

There had been no letter, no note or any kind of communication from Lady Landerbelt or Miss Newton at all, save for the invitation to Lady Huntington's ball, which had been sent with a note stating that Lady Landerbelt had requested specifically that they be able to attend. William had written back at once, accepting the invitation, all the while praying that this meant Lady Landerbelt still planned to help Olivia.

If only he had told them the truth about it all, instead of tucking it away and telling himself that there was nothing in it, then there would be no cause for this anxiety.

Lord Caversham scanned the ballroom, looking for Lady Landerbelt and Miss Newton. He knew that even catching a glimpse of Miss Newton would set his heart aflutter, but he certainly hoped that she would grant him an opportunity to write his name on her dance card.

"There she is," he heard Olivia whisper, her fingers tightening on his arm for a moment. "There, with Lord Winchester."

William felt his blood begin to boil before he'd so much as set eyes on Miss Newton, hating that she was once again in Lord Winchester's arms. Had he not explained himself well enough? Did she not know that Lord Winchester, more than Lord Dewford, was the reason behind the stain to his sister's good name?

"Calm yourself, Caversham," Olivia warned, clearly able to see the frustration and anger on his face. "Do not make yourself quite so obvious, my dear brother. They are sure to see you and comment on it."

He did not have to ask who "they" were, knowing full well that the *beau monde,* as one, would have beady eyes settling on them already. With an effort, he settled his shoulders, drew his eyes away from Miss Newton, and descended the stairs into the ballroom.

The ballroom was filled with lords and ladies. Some were dancing, others were strolling, and a few were huddled to the sides, deep in conversation. Despite the crowd, Lord Caversham never lost sight of Miss Newton. With each step, he felt himself growing increasingly anxious.

Then, to his horror, as he approached the last step, he saw Lord Winchester gesture towards him, saying something in Miss Newton's ear. Miss Newton then turned her head to glance over her shoulder at him, her eyes dancing, only to turn back and laugh, saying something to Lord Winchester to make him guffaw.

His skin prickled, his anger growing with every step. Miss Newton had turned her back on him, it seemed. Lord Winchester had apparently won her over, using his charm and affability to prove to her that he was the one telling the truth, not Olivia. He could barely contain himself, his heart slamming painfully into his chest as he tore his eyes away from her, feeling the biggest fool that ever walked in England.

"There is Lady Landerbelt," Olivia murmured, drawing her hand away. "She is beckoning me over."

"Go," he said, dully, dropping his arm.

Olivia paused. "Are you not coming?"

He could not speak, simply shaking his head and stepping away from her, making his way directly across the ballroom and out into the gardens. He was the foolish one, believing that there was something beginning to blossom between himself and Miss Newton, something that he was not quite sure what to do with, but now to see that he had been entirely wrong. She had been kind to him, yes, but that surely must have been only on her aunt's request. After what he had hidden from her as regarded Lord Winchester's brother, Miss Newton must have decided that he could not be trusted and had fallen entirely into the trap Lord Winchester had set for both her and any other young lady he could entice towards him.

It was all undone.

Feeling his heart tear apart within him and gasping from the pain of it all, William staggered down the steps into the gardens, finding a quiet place where he could simply sit and hide in the darkness. Moving past the lanterns, past the wooden benches that were near the French doors, he moved a little further back until he came across another bench, entirely shrouded in darkness and yet close enough to see the French doors and to hear the music. There he sat, his misery consuming him. He could not go back into the ballroom now, not when he knew that Lord Winchester and Miss Newton would be there, together. Lady Landerbelt might still be willing to help Olivia, and he would continue to thank her and support her in that, but he could not often be in Miss Newton's presence. It was too much too bear.

"My dear Lord Winchester, this is a little untoward!"

Grimacing, William threw his head in his hands as Miss Newton's voice came towards him, wondering if he was destined to be pursued by the lady despite his urge to get away from her.

"It is simply a quiet walk in the gardens," he heard Lord Winchester say, charmingly. "I can tell that you are a little flustered after our waltz, and I do so wish to aid you in recovering from that."

So, they were dancing a waltz. How wonderful for him.

William's thoughts grew more and more frequent as anger, scorn, and sheer frustration leached out of him. Clearly, he had felt more for Miss Newton than he had recognized, else he would not feel quite so upset.

"Indeed, I am glad of it, but I do not think we should stray far," Miss Newton said quietly. "Might we remain here, Lord

Winchester? I do not wish to walk any further, and the air is rather cool."

Aware that the benches Miss Newton and Lord Winchester were to sit on were very close to the stone bench he was currently using, William rolled his eyes and sent a prayer up to heaven that they would not see him, shifting a little farther along the bench as the cold stone seeped into his skin. If he could have made it possible, he would have crawled into the darkness beyond the bench simply to ensure that he could sit in his misery undetected.

"I would prefer we walk," Lord Winchester replied, with an almost purring tone to his voice. "Are you quite sure I cannot convince you?"

"Quite."

William was about to get up and leave, to move further into the shadows so that he would not even hear Miss Newton's voice, only for the harsh tone to catch him off-guard. In fact, Miss Newton did not sound in any way friendly or relaxed, and that in itself forced him to remain seated. Was she uncomfortable with the way Lord Winchester had cajoled her outside? Despite himself, despite the ongoing pain in his chest, William forced himself to remain still, a murmur of warning growing in his chest.

"I should tell you now, Miss Newton, I am a man used to getting what he wishes," Lord Winchester said, sounding a little irritated.

"And I am not inclined to bend," came the firm reply. "I will not walk, unchaperoned, in the gardens with you, Lord Winchester. Here, at least, we can see the door to the ballroom and those going in and out should be able to see us."

Lord Winchester chuckled darkly. "I did not think that a walk in the gardens required anyone to be able to see us, Miss Newton."

The warning in William's chest grew all the more.

"Fond as I am of you, Lord Winchester," came Miss Newton's rather chilly reply, "you will find that I do not give up my favors easily. Indeed, they must be earned."

"Earned?" Lord Winchester repeated, sounding both amused and intrigued. "And what must I do to earn them?"

There was a short pause, and William felt himself leaning forward in the darkness, desperate to catch every word that came from Miss Newton's lips.

"You must tell me something I wish to know," came the singsong reply, as though Miss Newton were playing a game. "Something that no one else knows."

Lord Winchester laughed aloud. "I do not have many secrets, Miss Newton."

"I believe you do," Miss Newton retorted. "After all, I am quite sure that you had Lord Darnley walk with Lady Olivia on the night of Lord Bradford's ball. Did you know that she had the pendant then?" Her tone became filled with admiration. "Did you set it all up so that you would be able to declare her as the thief?"

William could hardly breathe, suddenly sickened by what he had heard. Miss Newton believed Olivia to be guilty. The truth was so clear to him that it almost knocked him backwards, feeling the life drain out of his limbs. Miss Newton did not care for Olivia, and clearly, regardless of what her aunt thought, she believed her to be the thief that the rest of society thought she was.

It was as if she'd reached in, taken his heart in her hands, and torn it into tiny pieces, dropping each piece to the floor in a bloodied mess. He didn't know what to think, nor what to do, remaining fixed on the garden bench as Miss Newton continued with her merry conversation.

Lord Winchester chuckled darkly. "You are far too perceptive, Miss Newton, but if it will grant me a favor with you, then I shall admit it. Yes, I used Lord Darnley for the express purpose you stated – and it worked wonderfully well, did it not?"

"It did indeed!" Miss Newton exclaimed, sounding overcome with wonder. "It is just a shame that Lord Bradford did not instantly believe you, as you had hoped. How terrible it must be for you to know the truth and yet have the gentleman who was almost stolen from refuse to believe you! He did not even thank you, I am sure!"

There was a short pause. "No, he did not," Lord Winchester agreed, sounding almost downcast. "I am quite sure there will be a way to prove that Lady Olivia is exactly who I know her to be, but I have yet to think of one. There was no necklace recovered in Lord Caversham's home, as you know, but I am certain that is because she has moved it elsewhere."

There was another pause, as though Miss Newton was thinking, hard. William wanted to explode upon them both, to scream and decry them both in equal measure, but he found his limbs too weak to move.

"Mayhap I might be able to help you there, Lord Winchester," Miss Newton continued, in a rather eager tone. "Then the *ton* would know that you were right to blame Lady Olivia; they will declare you a hero, and then all will be as it should be."

Lord Winchester cleared his throat. "What is it you are thinking, Miss Newton?"

"Well," Miss Newton continued eagerly. "I am still acquainted with Lady Olivia, as we both thought best, and there might be a way I could use that to our advantage."

"What do you mean?" Lord Winchester asked, sounding intrigued. "You think you might be able to persuade her to reveal the necklace?"

"I could try."

There came another long pause, and William felt strength return to his limbs, forcing himself to stand despite the trembling in his knees.

"If she did, then it would prove to all and sundry that she did take the ruby necklace from Lady Edgeware, and then your story about finding her with the pendant will be shown to be true," Miss Newton declared. "Now, how about it?"

"Let me think on it," came the swift reply. "I do agree that it is, in itself, a marvelous idea, and I am truly delighted in your willingness to aid me, but such a plan must be given deep consideration."

Miss Newton let out a small, delighted laugh, as William began to stagger towards them. "But of course, Lord Winchester! We shall put our heads together and prove to the *ton* that you are a truly wonderful gentleman, who deserves much praise and honor for what he has done in revealing this dire truth about Lady Olivia."

Lord Winchester swaggered a little as he walked away, with Miss Newton on his arm. William was too late to catch them and was forced to draw in long, deep breaths as he tried to calm his furious anger.

"Indeed, I do deserve all that you have said, and more!" he agreed, as he and Miss Newton climbed the steps towards the French doors. "Now, what favor shall you bestow on me since I have now answered all of your questions?"

Miss Newton laughed again, the sound tearing at William's soul. "Why, my dear Lord Winchester, you will simply have to wait and see!"

8

The following morning William awoke in his townhouse and found that he could barely lift his head from the pillow, such was his torment. He had not known what to say to Olivia, who had appeared from the ballroom with such delight in her features that he could not bring himself to tear that from her. Instead, he had remained silent, muttering something about a headache when she asked him why he was so quiet.

Pushing himself up in bed, he accepted the breakfast tray and then requested that he be left in peace, only for the butler to appear at the door.

"My lord, I do not wish to disturb you, but Lady Olivia sent me to remind you that Lady Landerbelt is due to visit this afternoon."

Does Lady Landerbelt know of what Miss Newton is doing? he asked himself, as the butler waited patiently. *Will she come too, so that she can discern what it is we are planning to do?*

"My lord?" the butler said, a little more gently. "Should I inform her that you will be absent from the afternoon call?"

"No."

There was nothing more to be said. The butler nodded, with

just a slight flicker of worry crossing his brow before he shut the door, leaving William alone.

Sighing heavily, William rubbed at his forehead, feeling the beginnings of a headache. He had drunk far too much last evening on his return from the ball, overwhelmed with dismay and horror at what had come from Miss Newton's lips. He did not know what to say to Olivia, still entirely confused over whether or not Lady Landerbelt knew of her niece's intentions with Lord Winchester.

"Then perhaps she *ought* to know if she does not already," he muttered to himself, picking up a slice of toast. "And we shall have nothing more to do with Miss Newton from this moment on."

A sudden thought occurred to him and, reaching for the bell pull, William waited impatiently for the footman to arrive.

"Send a note to Lady Landerbelt at once," he said, before the footman could so much as open his mouth. "State that we wish to see her and her alone. Miss Newton is not invited."

The footman goggled at him for a moment, making William all the more exasperated.

"By golly, I shall write it myself," he exclaimed, as the footman hurried to take the breakfast tray so he might throw the covers back to climb out of bed. "Set that tray by the fire."

"At once, my lord," the footman muttered, clearly a little confused by William's brusque manner – not that William cared a jot about what his staff thought. Sitting down at his writing desk, he picked up his quill and quickly wrote a short and rather blunt note, making it clear that he did not wish Miss Newton to be present at their afternoon meeting. Should she have the temerity to appear at his door regardless, demanding to know why she was no longer invited into his home, William would take great delight in declaring all that he knew in front of anyone who happened to be present.

"Here," he said, thrusting the note at the footman. "And there is no need to wait for a response."

A small smile curved his lips as the footman hurried from the room, note in hand. There was a small sense of satisfaction creeping through him as he sat back down to eat his breakfast, glad that he would never have to lay eyes on the scheming Miss Newton again.

SOME HOURS later and William marched into the drawing room, expecting to see only Olivia as the time for Lady Landerbelt's visit had not yet drawn near. He was dressed and coiffed to perfection, his shoulders lifted and head held high. Miss Newton might have thought that she was keeping her liaison with Lord Winchester a secret, but he knew it all now. The truth would be out, and it would be to her shame.

However, Lady Landerbelt was already present in the drawing room and did not rise as he came in, her brows furrowed. Olivia herself appeared to be rather startled, her eyes wide as William came into the room, clearly unaware of what had passed between the two houses earlier that day.

"Lady Landerbelt," William said, almost grandly as he bowed. "How good of you to grace us with your presence."

"Lord Caversham," Lady Landerbelt replied, with a slight frown. "I was a little perturbed to receive your note earlier this afternoon. Is there something the matter?"

"Direct as always, Lady Landerbelt," William replied, seating himself across from Lady Landerbelt and ignoring the startled look on Olivia's face. "But yes, there is something particularly grave that has occurred and, as yet, I am unaware of just how much you know of this matter."

"Caversham," Olivia breathed, sitting forward in her seat.

"Whatever is the matter? Why are you looking so grave? Is this from last evening?"

"Last evening at the ball?" Lady Landerbelt repeated, looking a little surprised. "If there was something concerning there, Lord Caversham, I should have been glad to know of it then."

He arched a brow, sitting back in his chair as the maids brought in the tea trays. There was a slow-growing tension settling over all of them, made all the more intense by the fact that the maids were present. It was only once they had closed the door behind them that William began to speak.

"I was rather surprised to see Miss Newton with Lord Winchester last evening, Lady Landerbelt," he began. "They were dancing, talking and laughing with such delight that it is as though they are very well acquainted – and intend to pursue that acquaintance even further."

To his astonishment, Lady Landerbelt simply laughed and waved a hand. "Oh, goodness, Lord Caversham! If that is all that troubles you, then let me put your mind at ease. I—"

"That is not all, Lady Landerbelt," William continued firmly. "Did you know that your niece intends to prove that Olivia is, in fact, guilty of the crimes she supposedly did?"

Olivia gasped, one hand over her mouth as Lady Landerbelt frowned, her laughter gone in an instant.

"Indeed, I heard her talking with Lord Winchester last evening," he continued, feeling almost proud of himself with each word that passed his lips. "They are to prove that Olivia stole the ruby necklace by somehow forcing her to present it to Miss Newton. I have no doubt that the lady herself will fetch it from Lord Winchester, or Lord Dewford – whomever has it – and make it appear that it was, in fact, Olivia who presented it to her."

Lady Landerbelt's frown deepened all the more. "Lord Caversham, do you truly think so little of my niece?"

A stab of pain sliced through his heart. "It does not matter what I think, Lady Landerbelt, but what I *know* that matters. And I know what passed between your niece and Lord Winchester last evening. Now, the question is, how much do you yourself know?"

Lady Landerbelt lifted her chin, her eyes flashing dangerously. "You believe that I, in fact, might be working alongside Miss Newton to prove that Lady Olivia is guilty? For what reason, might I ask? I, who have been the place your sister now stands, would turn on her for no other reason than to please Lord Winchester? Is that what you think?"

Sand filled William's mouth as he struggled to answer. He had gone too far. Of course, Lady Landerbelt had not been involved with her niece. It was much too ridiculous to suggest.

"No, of course he does not think that." He heard Olivia say the words, as his shoulders slumped. "Truly, Lady Landerbelt, I had no notion that he thought any of this. I am utterly astonished."

Lady Landerbelt gave Olivia a faint smile and patted her hand, before directing her steely gaze back onto William. She picked up her cup from the tray and took a small sip of tea before setting the cup back down again. Her gaze never wavered from the face of Lord Caversham while completed the motion.

"I should not have suggested such a thing about you, Lady Landerbelt," he admitted, no longer feeling as delighted with himself as he had been. "I apologize."

"And you can think of no other reason for my niece to have such a conversation with Lord Winchester?" Lady Landerbelt asked, a trifle more gently. "No? Then I suggest you speak to her yourself."

He looked up at her sharply. "I made it clear that I do not want Miss Newton to set foot in this house."

"And I have ignored your request," Lady Landerbelt replied pointedly. "I came a little early and directed Miss Newton to arrive at the proper time. She will be here at any moment."

All of a sudden, William felt as though he had burst into flame. The heat was tearing through him, a flush burning from his neck up into his cheeks. He did not know what to say or do, suddenly terrified at the thought of seeing Miss Newton again. He did not want to have those same feelings begin to course through him once more, not when she had betrayed them both so terribly.

"No," he said, firmly, shaking his head. "I will not—"

"Yes, you will, William."

Startled, William looked up to see Olivia standing tall, her eyes burning holes into his skin.

"You will allow Miss Newton to enter, and you will have a *civil* conversation about whatever it is you have heard," she continued, showing more strength and temerity than he had ever expected from her. "I, for one, do not believe that there is anything in it. Whatever you heard, there was a reason behind it. I trust Lady Landerbelt and Miss Newton entirely."

And that is to your downfall, William thought to himself, struck dumb by the ferocity on Olivia's face.

"Very well," he said begrudgingly, as she took her seat. "But only because you ask it of me, Olivia. Not because I believe that she in any way deserves it." He was aware that he was being both harsh and disrespectful, but given his tumultuous feelings, William did not care. His sister glared at him, her cheeks now a rosy red as she tried to turn away from where he sat, clearly embarrassed.

"Be careful, Lord Caversham," Lady Landerbelt said again,

although much more gently this time. "You may come to regret your words."

He did not reply but sat up straight, his shoulders flat and hands in his lap. He did not move or speak, not even when Olivia began to make sincere apologies for him, which Lady Landerbelt accepted gently, sending disappointed looks in his direction. With every passing moment, he felt his anxiety rise all the higher within him. What would he say to her when she arrived? She, who had haunted his thoughts ever since they had first laid eyes on one another and who had gone on to betray Olivia so terribly? His stomach knotted, his palms growing sweaty as his eyes continued to stray towards the door, wondering when it might open.

Finally, the butler appeared in the doorway and William rose to his feet.

"Miss Newton, my lord," the butler said, as Miss Newton came into the room behind him.

"How lovely to see you again," she exclaimed, a bright smile on her face as she made her way over to them all. "It has been some days since we last saw one another, and I will confess to missing you both!"

Stepping deliberately into her path, William glared at the lady he'd once thought so much about, his hands planted firmly on his hips.

"Lord Caversham?" she said, looking a little uncertain. "Is everything all right?"

His lips thinned, his heart beating frantically in his chest as he took her in. "No, Miss Newton, everything is not quite all right."

"I'm afraid Lord Caversham believes you to be in league with Lord Winchester, my dear," Lady Landerbelt said in a heavy voice. "Apparently you were overheard last evening."

William watched with satisfaction as Miss Newton's face

went sheet white, her eyes widening as she looked back at him. Clearly, she had not expected to be caught.

"Oh dear," she murmured, shaking her head. And then, to his utter surprise, her lip curved upwards, and she gave him a small half smile. "My dear Lord Caversham, whatever have you assumed about me, I can assure you that you are quite wrong in this matter."

"Wrong?" he spluttered, feeling as though he were drifting hopelessly out at sea, being entirely confused as to why Miss Newton should appear to be so delighted. "I know what I over-heard, Miss Newton."

She sighed then, rather heavily and shook her head. "My dear Lord Caversham, you have misunderstood entirely. Now, if you will allow me to explain, then I shall start at the beginning."

Lady Landerbelt rose from her seat.

"Come, Olivia. Let us leave Miss Newton and your *dear* brother to themselves. I do not want to be in the room during what I am sure will be a rather loud argument." She lifted one eyebrow towards William, her eyes filled with something akin to frustration, although there was a small smile playing around her cheeks.

"Aunt," Miss Newton replied with a little irritation. "I do not think that there will be any kind of argument. You need not leave."

Lady Landerbelt lifted her chin, her eyes piercing William. "I think it best, Catherine. Do excuse us. Olivia, let us take a walk in your brother's garden."

William remained standing, as Olivia walked with Lady Landerbelt out of his drawing room, leaving him standing alone with Miss Newton. It was a little improper, but he did not partic-ularly care about such things at the moment. Lifting his chin, he gazed steadily at Miss Newton, recalling every single word she had said to Lord Winchester the night before.

"Well, Miss Newton," he began harshly, as the door was left a little ajar behind Lady Landerbelt. "How are you to explain what you said to Lord Winchester? How are you to convince me that you are still to accept my court, whilst sharing your favors with Lord Winchester? I may have been fooled once, Miss Newton, but I will not be so fooled again."

Miss Newton frowned, the light in her eyes fading as she looked back at him. Then, without warning, she stepped forward and kissed him, hard.

William could not help but respond.

9

Catherine was not quite sure what she was doing, but the urge to press her lips to Lord Caversham's had grown so strong within her that she had been unable to prevent herself from doing just that.

Everything was a blur. She was hardly able to breathe, such was the tightness with which Lord Caversham had pulled her full against him but found that being held so closely was sending waves of heat all through her. Lord Caversham was kissing her back with such an intensity that it almost felt rather fierce. His hands were roaming over the small of her back, and she found that her own fingers were now tangled in his hair.

And then, without warning, Lord Caversham stepped back, dropping his hands from her and lowering his head.

Catherine struggled to catch her breath, her eyes widening as she looked back at Lord Caversham, who was still unable to raise his gaze to hers.

"Do not tempt me so, Miss Newton," he said gruffly. "I cannot allow myself to be taken in, not if you have plans to bring pain to my sister."

Her heart broke. Not because he doubted her but because of

the sheer pain that was wracked all through him. His expression was one of confusion, of grief, and she could not help but go to him.

"Lord Caversham, you are quite mistaken," she murmured, walking over towards him and taking his hand in her own. He did not look at her still, although their hands remained joined. "I am sorry that you overheard my conversation with Lord Winchester."

His heart jerked up. "I was not supposed to hear it, was I?"

She gave him a small, sad smile, feeling her heart tear yet again. "Oh, Caversham," she said softly, lifting her other hand to brush the side of his face gently. "If I had been able to speak to you before Lord Winchester had taken me out to the gardens, then you would not be so hurt." Shaking her head, she drew him towards the chairs and, seating herself down carefully on one, waited until he had sat down also. His eyes did not meet hers, his head still low as he gazed at the floor. Pulling his hand out of her own, he sat with his hands folded in his lap, refusing to look at her.

"Lord Caversham, what you heard me say to Lord Winchester in the gardens during the ball last evening was nothing more than a ruse," she explained softly. "It is something that Aunt Angelica and I have not yet had the opportunity to share with you – indeed, we thought it best not to share it for a time."

Slowly, his head began to lift.

"It was, perhaps, a little cruel, but we had to make sure that Lord Winchester believed that I had turned my affections towards him, that I believed every word he was saying. It was for that reason that we did not share the truth about what was going on with you. I do hope you can forgive me."

"You do not know what it was like," came the hoarse reply. "What it was like to enter into the ballroom and see you with that man. The man who has brought so much trouble to my sister. You were dancing and laughing with him, and my heart was torn from my chest."

Swallowing the lump in her throat, Catherine reached for Lord Caversham's hand again and, to her relief, he allowed her to take it.

"It was all a façade," she promised, praying that he would believe her. "I do not care one jot for Lord Winchester. I find him to be arrogant, self-centered, and so filled with pride that it is difficult for me to so much as smile at him!" A small sigh escaped her. "And yet I must, for the sake of your sister."

With a great slowness, Lord Caversham's eyes lifted to hers, and Catherine caught her breath at the pain that was so deep within them. She did not feel anger towards him for thinking what he had, understanding *why* he had believed her to be so double minded.

"I know that Lord Winchester has done this to Lady Olivia," she continued softly, "and I believe my aunt has a theory as to why. However, in order to prove that it was he who took the ruby necklace and he who took the pendant, only to frame Olivia, we must come up with a plan whereby he is forced to produce the ruby necklace. He will try, of course, to make it look as though Olivia has had it in her possession ever since its disappearance, but we will catch him out."

"How will we be able to catch him out?"

Lord Caversham's words were low and heavy, as though filled with a great hopelessness that she could not quite break through.

"We will find a way," Catherine promised, desperate for him to look at her, for him to smile and believe that all would be well. "My aunt has some things to explain to you, Lord Caversham – I mean, to explain to all of us, for I do not know all that she has been up to this last while, and I am quite certain that she has a plan. Do you think you can trust her, Lord Caversham? Do you think you might be able to, once again, trust me?"

Her fingers pleated the fabric of her gown anxiously as she waited for Lord Caversham's response, seeing the way he lowered his head again. There was nothing but silence for a few minutes, and Catherine felt tears begin to prick at the corner of her eyes as she waited, terrified that Lord Caversham would turn away from her now, that he would not believe what she had told him.

"I have been all kinds of a fool."

Letting out a long breath, Catherine closed her eyes and tried not to let the tears fall but felt the moisture on her cheeks regardless. A handkerchief was pressed to them and, as she opened her eyes, she saw Lord Caversham looking back at her with a deep concern, guilt and shame written across his face.

"My dear Miss Newton," he whispered hoarsely. "Can you ever forgive me?"

She swallowed hard.

"I am so terribly sorry for all that I thought, for all that I have said," he continued, shaking his head. "I was confused. I thought that you—" He broke off and turned away. "Forgive me, Miss Newton."

There was no hesitation on her part. Capturing his face with her hands, she waited until he'd lifted his grief-stricken eyes towards hers, wanting to put an end to his pain.

"Lord Caversham, you are more than forgiven," she promised, tears springing into her eyes anew. "I am sorry we did not speak to you about our plans for Lord Winchester before now. If we had, then perhaps this might not have occurred."

His lips turned down. "I ought never to have doubted you, Miss Newton. My heart has been so filled with you that it was as if it had been taken from me and ripped apart. I thought...."

She smiled at him, despite the tears falling from her eyes

still. "No, Lord Caversham, I still have every intention of being courted by you once this whole, terrible mess comes to a close. That is, if you still wish to court me! I confess that my heart is already filled with such a deep affection for you that I cannot turn away from you now."

Watching Lord Caversham, she saw him close his eyes for a moment as a long, shuddering sigh left his lips.

"I do not deserve such an affection, Miss Newton," he said hoarsely. "And yet my own foolish heart is filled with no one but you."

Her smile grew, her heart leaping for joy within her. "Then I think you must call me 'Catherine,' Lord Caversham. For we are, it seems, already on the path towards courtship."

Finally, a small smile curved his lips, as he looked into her eyes, his fingers trailing lightly down her cheek. "Then 'Catherine' it shall be," he murmured, before leaning in to kiss her once more.

"WELL, I would not call that much of an argument!"

Relieved that they had managed to step apart before Aunt Angelica had re-entered the room, Catherine smiled demurely as Aunt Angelica sent her a piercing look before training her gaze on Lord Caversham, who was standing a few steps away.

"We heard no shouting at all," Aunt Angelica continued, arching a brow as she came to sit down. "Is all resolved between you?"

Catherine nodded. "It is."

"Very good." One more sharp look towards Lord Caversham told Catherine that Aunt Angelica knew very well what had gone on between them, although she could not tell whether or not this pleased her aunt or not.

"Then I do hope, Lord Caversham, that you will soon come

to me with a question about continuing your acquaintance with my niece," Lady Angelica said with a firmness to her voice. "You understand my meaning, I am sure."

Lord Caversham flushed but inclined his head. "Of course, Lady Landerbelt. I have every intention of doing so once Olivia is settled."

The smallest of smiles caught Lady Landerbelt's lips as she nodded, turning her gaze back towards Catherine. "Very good. Very good. Well, then, now that we are all here, I think I should inform you about what I have discovered of late."

Catherine sat forward as maids appeared with a fresh teapot and more cups on a tray. They set the tray on the nearby table, taking the old tray with the cold teapot and cups away, before departing from Lord Caversham's drawing room. "What is it, Aunt Angelica?"

A broad smile settled on her aunt's face. "Well, my dear, I have discovered that Lord Winchester's brother has passed away."

Glancing over at Lord Caversham, Catherine saw him frown.

"I was talking to one of my new friends, who has become very dear to me of late since she is *such* a gossip," Lady Landerbelt continued, "and she informed me that Lord Winchester's brother was fished out of the Thames some time ago."

"Goodness," Catherine murmured, one hand on her heart. "How awful."

Lady Landerbelt waved a hand. "Indeed, indeed. However, what is most interesting to me is that Lord Winchester apparently took very badly to this. He did not want to believe what most people suggested – that either the man had lost his footing and tumbled in headfirst, given that he was well known to be a man who drank often but yet could not hold his liquor, or that he had done so deliberately."

"Either way, it is a terrible tragedy," Lady Olivia said softly, looking almost distraught. "That poor gentleman."

Lady Landerbelt nodded. "You have a kind heart, Lady Olivia, I must say. I, however, am a little more detached, I think." There was a short pause as she shrugged. "Perhaps it is because I have been forced to build a wall around my heart, given what I have experienced."

Catherine frowned, seeing the slight worry in her aunt's face as she talked. It was true that Aunt Angelica had been through a very great deal but was she truly worried that it had closed herself off in some way? That did not seem apparent to Catherine, of course, but then again she could not see into the depths of her aunt's heart.

Giving herself a slight shake, Lady Landerbelt turned to Lady Olivia with a gentle smile. "This is not any of your doing, Olivia, so you are not to take any of this onto yourself – and nor are you, Lord Caversham, but I believe that Lord Winchester decided that the person to blame for his brother's untimely death was you."

There came a gasp from Olivia, and Lady Landerbelt took her hand at once, all the while keeping her gaze on Lord Caversham.

"I believe that he has since then dedicated himself into making your life a misery," she continued, gently. "That campaign has focused on Olivia and, in time, I am sure will turn onto you. He intends to take all he can from you, without putting any blame onto himself."

"But why?" Catherine asked, her throat working hard as she saw the tears form in Olivia's eyes. "He believes that his brother's death was due to Lord Caversham's refusal to allow him to wed Olivia? Is that all?"

Lady Landerbelt nodded, still training her gaze on Lord Caversham. "I believe so. We will have to prove it, of course."

Lord Caversham cleared his throat, shooting a glance towards Catherine. "And how might we do that?"

Catherine watched as her aunt appeared to brighten almost at once, her hand tightening on Lady Olivia's.

"Well, now that you are aware of my niece's involvement with Lord Winchester, I confess that I have come up with an idea that I hope will prove to sort everything out in a matter of minutes."

There was a short pause, and Catherine rolled her eyes in her aunt's direction, sitting back in her chair with a small smile before recalling that she was meant to be pouring the tea. It was quite clear that her aunt was hesitating for an almost dramatic effect, which she had no need to do given just how severe the situation already was.

"Thank you, Catherine," Aunt Angelica murmured as she accepted the cup of tea. "Yes, of course, I have a plan. Catherine, you shall tell Lord Winchester that Lady Olivia broke down in front of you the moment you began to discuss the ruby necklace. You shall tell him that she confessed all to you. Declare to him that Lady Olivia is terribly confused by it all and that she does not remember what she did that evening. You have promised her that you will go with her to that particular room – the one you chose to rest in at the time of the ball – just in case something comes back to her there." She chuckled, shaking her head. "I am quite sure that Lord Winchester will see the opportunity and grasp it with both hands. You must make sure to tell him, Catherine, that you intend to go there with her during Lady Edgeware's evening recital in three days' time – which has all been arranged with Lady Edgeware herself. Lord Winchester has, of course, been invited also."

Catherine frowned, handing a cup to Lady Olivia. "But what is the point of returning to the room where Olivia was resting prior to all of this? I do not understand what it will achieve."

"Do you not see?" Lady Landerbelt exclaimed, her eyes bright. "It gives Lord Winchester the perfect opportunity to hide the ruby necklace in the room and then 'discover' it again, in order to declare Olivia's guilt."

There were a few minutes of silence following this statement as each one thought hard about what Lady Landerbelt had suggested.

"And do you truly believe that Lord Winchester will be taken in by this, Lady Landerbelt?" Olivia asked, looking rather afraid. "If he does not, then..."

Lord Caversham cleared his throat, looking in Catherine's direction. "Lord Winchester is arrogance himself. He believes that he has gotten away with the things he has done thus far, in declaring Olivia to be the guilty one, and yet has not quite managed to prove it to anyone. I think, given how much he is interested in Catherine – I mean, Miss Newton – that he will believe what she has to say and will do exactly as you hope, Lady Landerbelt."

"We can but hope," Lady Landerbelt replied firmly. "Now, Olivia, you must go with Catherine when I give you the signal. Lord Caversham, you are not to be invited to Lady Edgeware's evening recital, but you are to be there regardless. Hidden in the room, so that you might be able to appear when needed. But do not make yourself known until Lord Winchester's guilt has been declared."

Still a little unsure as to what was going on, Catherine sent a small, wry smile towards Lord Caversham, which he returned at once. They were going to have to trust Lady Landerbelt and hope that this would, in the end, bring the whole nasty business to a very satisfactory conclusion.

"Catherine, we must go," Lady Landerbelt finished, getting to her feet. "We have a meeting that I cannot be late for."

Surprised, Catherine rose and looked over at her aunt, who was smiling brightly. "A meeting, Aunt?"

"Yes, indeed," Lady Landerbelt declared, patting Olivia's hand. "With one Lord Darnley, in fact. No, he is not expecting us, but I know where he is to be. Do come along."

Turning to Lord Caversham, Catherine smiled as he took her hand and pressed it to his lips.

"I shall see you in three days' time, Lord Caversham," she murmured, as his mouth pressed a gentle kiss to the back of her hand. "And then all will be settled."

His eyes were warm as he smiled back at her. "Indeed it will."

10

I gnoring her niece's startled look, Angelica walked into Lady Edgeware's drawing room and greeted her old friend with a great deal of warmth. Catherine took in the blues and golds that adorned the room. The royal blue chairs really seemed to pop in contrast to the gold surrounding the perfectly shined mirror.

"My dear Lady Landerbelt," Lady Edgeware declared. "I am truly delighted to have you call. After your very strange notes of late, I confess myself to be rather intrigued as to what it is you are up to!"

Laughing, Angelica stepped out of the way and introduced Catherine, who greeted Lady Edgeware with a slightly confused smile.

"I can see that you are at as much of a loss as I," Lady Edgeware chuckled, as Catherine sat down in one of the brilliant chairs.

"Indeed, I am," Catherine replied, looking over at Angelica for a moment. "I did not know that my aunt was acquainted with you, Lady Edgeware."

Lady Edgeware waved a hand. "Oh, we were debutantes

together a few years ago, Miss Newton, although we did lose touch when your aunt married and went away."

"And it is all the better to have returned to London and seen you again," Angelica replied warmly. "I must thank you for all you have done of late. I know my requests have seemed very strange and you have not once questioned me."

She had written to Lady Edgeware almost the moment she had met Olivia and had visited the day after, simply to hear the story from Lady Edgeware herself. The lady had been distraught that the ruby necklace had gone missing and was truly beside herself with the notion that Lady Olivia, a lady so proper and refined, could have taken it for herself. Angelica had talked at length about Lady Olivia, to the point that Lady Edgeware had finally agreed that there was, in fact, a chance that Lady Olivia was not guilty of what Lord Dewford had accused her of. Lady Edgeware even went so far as to agree that she and her husband were inclined to believe Lord Dewford's testimony over Lady Olivia's, simply because he was known to Lady Edgeware's husband, Viscount Edgeware. Since then, Angelica had sent a series of notes to Lady Edgeware, requesting that she organize an evening recital and to make sure to invite certain ladies and gentlemen. It was, she promised, an attempt to retrieve the ruby necklace and, to her very great relief, Lady Edgeware had agreed.

"Now then," Lady Edgeware said briskly, smoothing her green gown and looking at Angelica with her intense blue eyes, her brows a little furrowed. "What is it that you are planning for this evening recital, Lady Landerbelt? And what is it that you require me to do?"

Angelica smiled, taking in her friend's severe expression and glad that she had been so willing. "My dear Lady Edgeware, all you must do is ensure that the room Lady Olivia was resting in that night of the ball is thoroughly searched by your footmen, with you or your husband overseeing their search."

Lady Edgeware frowned, tucking back a small dark curl behind her ear. "Search the room, Lady Landerbelt? You believe my necklace to be there?"

"No, I do not," Angelica explained, laughing softly as she saw both Catherine and Lady Edgeware's confusion. "But you must be certain that the necklace is not there, and you must have a footman on hand to attest to it when the time comes."

Lady Edgeware nodded slowly, her brow still furrowed. "Very well."

"And, if I might be so bold as to ask, might you be willing to leave the recital for a time and come to that particular room at a time of my choosing?" Angelica continued, aware that her niece was now frowning heavily. "The true thief will be revealed."

A startled gasp from Catherine caught Angelica's attention and, as she looked over at her niece, she saw Catherine's eyes sparkle with a sudden delight. Clearly, her niece had worked out what it was she intended to do.

"And I will have my ruby necklace back?" Lady Edgeware asked, not glancing over at Catherine. "Without a doubt?"

"Without a doubt," Angelica replied firmly, ignoring the slight niggle of worry in her mind. This would only work if Lord Winchester was convinced that this opportunity was ripe for the taking. She had to pray that Catherine could continue to flatter the man, just as she had done before.

Lady Edgeware sighed and spread her hands. "Very well."

"One more thing I must ask of you," Angelica continued, a little more hastily. "I must ask you to declare Lady Olivia's innocence to anyone who will listen once the matter is settled. The *ton* must know that she has been treated very unfairly."

Slowly, Lady Edgeware nodded, her eyes sharp. "I suppose I must trust you on this, Lady Landerbelt, since you have promised to retrieve my necklace. Of course, if the lady is innocent, then I shall do all I can for her!"

"Thank you," Angelica replied quietly. "That is wonderful to hear, Lady Edgeware."

Her friend frowned but nodded, shrugging her shoulders as though she did not quite understand but was willing to do what she was asked regardless. This was something Angelica was more than grateful for, although she had slowly begun to realize that her influence on society was greater than ever before. To be declared a murderess, only to then be shown to be innocent made her the object of interest to a great many people, although she was not sure she liked such attention. At least, however, it granted her entry to anywhere and everywhere, with the *beau monde* almost desperate to have her presence. For a moment, her thoughts flitted to Lord Thorndyke, wondering what he made of her new status within society, only for a knock at the door to catch her attention and drag her back to the present.

"This will be your visitor, Lady Landerbelt," Lady Edgeware murmured, as the door opened. "I have a footman ready."

Angelica rose to her feet, just as a tall, dark-haired gentlemen with a slightly confused expression on his face stepped into the room. His eyes drifted form Lady Edgeware to Catherine to Angelica – and then something in his expression changed. He looked almost terrified, his eyes widening and his cheeks going pale.

"Ah, Lord Darnley, thank you for responding to my request for you to call," Lady Edgeware said grandly. "Do come in."

Lord Darnley shook his head. "I do apologize, Lady Edgeware, but I realize now that I have made an error in coming here. I must be going."

"Going?" Angelica asked, arching an eyebrow as the gentleman stepped towards the door, only for a footman to step directly in front of it. "I did not think you would be as rude as all this, Lord Darnley!"

"Rude?" Lord Darnley repeated, turning back around. "I do not know what you mean."

"Come now," Angelica said, cajolingly. "You must be aware of why you are here, Lord Darnley, and I can assure you that I will not allow you to leave until you tell me everything."

Lord Darnley swallowed, hard, his eyes still wide and his hands twisting together as he looked back at them all.

"You know that I am dear friends with Lady Olivia, do you not?" Angelica asked, a little more softly, as the man gave her his full attention. "And you know that you had something to do with Lady Olivia's supposed theft of the pendant. That is why you appear so afraid."

Lord Darnley's jaw worked for a moment, but he lifted his chin and turned away. "I know nothing about that."

Angelica chuckled darkly, aware that the man's demeanor gave more away than he intended. "Lord Darnley, I do not believe a word of it. Now you will tell me everything, and I will make it worth your while for you to do so. You are in a great deal of debt, I believe." She glanced back to Lady Edgeware, who nodded firmly. "My dear friend, Lady Edgeware, has found out as much about you as she can, so you need not deny it, Lord Darnley. Now, come and sit down and tell me what Lord Winchester requested of you."

Lord Darnley appeared to be some kind of trapped animal, his eyes darting from place to place in an attempt to find a way to escape. Angelica, knowing that she could not allow him to leave, sighed heavily and gestured towards the empty chair. "There is nowhere for you to go, Lord Darnley. I suggest you tell me everything and, as I said, I will make it worth your while."

"But Lord Winchester, he..." Lord Darnley trailed off, aware that he had said too much as his eyes widened even further.

Angelica's smile spread across her face, a feeling of satisfaction settling in her soul. She had him now. "Lord Darnley, I assure you that you have nothing to be anxious about when it comes to Lord Winchester. In fact, I would suggest that you would be better off distancing yourself from the gentleman as much as you can."

Catherine cleared her throat, lifting her chin as she gazed back at Lord Darnley, her resolve as steady as Angelica's. "Lord Winchester is to be rejected by society in a few days' time, Lord Darnley. Do you wish to be thrown aside with him?"

There was a long pause until, finally, Lord Darnley shook his head.

"Very good," Angelica said, firmly. "Then you must tell us everything that occurred, Lord Darnley, from the very beginning."

11

"When do you go?"

Catherine tried to giggle, as though she were playing some kind of marvelous game as Lord Winchester sidled up to her. He had been delighted to hear of Catherine's news and had agreed wholeheartedly that she ought to aid Lady Olivia in trying to remember what had taken place. Catherine had been forced to endure his nearness as they had talked only yesterday during a walk through the streets of London, having to play the part of an adoring young debutante, who was entirely caught up by his charms.

Lord Winchester had been equally delighted to discover that both Lady Olivia and Catherine were to attend Lady Edgeware's evening recital, telling Catherine that it would be her best opportunity to take Lady Olivia back to that room in the hope she could remember what she had done that night.

"I shall take her very soon, I think," Catherine whispered back, hating that he was carefully leading her backwards towards the shadowy corners of the room. "When there is a short break for refreshments."

Lord Winchester rubbed his hands. "A capital idea."

"Where will you be?" she asked, looking up into his face and deciding that he was really a very cruel-looking man despite his handsome features. "Might you come with us?"

He nodded slowly. "I think a few minutes after you have entered will be enough," he agreed, taking her hand in his. "Lady Olivia will be startled, of course, and will pretend not to know what it is I am speaking of, but I am certain we will find the necklace within the room somewhere. That is, of course, why no one found the necklace in Lord Caversham's home. The stupid girl must have left the necklace here in a fit of panic, and then could not say a word to anyone!"

Catherine sighed and smiled up at him sweetly. "You have quite a remarkable mind on you, Lord Winchester. I am quite sure it is just as you say." There came a lull in the music, and she looked over to see Lady Edgeware rising to her feet to declare that there would be a short break and that refreshments were to be served in the dining room. Almost the moment she finished speaking, Lady Olivia also rose and began to look about anxiously, just as Lady Landerbelt had instructed her to do.

"I must go," Catherine whispered, pressing Lord Winchester's hand. "She is waiting for me."

Lord Winchester chuckled, leaned down, and pressed a kiss to Catherine's cheek – which she struggled not to recoil from.

"Lord Winchester!" she exclaimed, stepping back from him whilst trying to put on a faint smile. "You ought not to be so improper."

He laughed again and shook his head. "You did promise me some of your favors, Miss Newton, did you not? After Lady Olivia has been declared a thief, I shall come in search of you immediately so as to finally claim them for my own."

She flushed with anger and embarrassment, which Lord Winchester appeared to take as nothing more than a blush.

"It will be over very soon, I am sure," Catherine managed to say, before turning her back on him and making her way towards Lady Olivia.

"Are you within, Lord Caversham?"

Catherine's whisper echoed around the room, as Olivia clung to her hand. There was no response for a moment or two, only for the drawn curtains to suddenly move and Lord Caversham to appear from behind them.

"Yes, I am here," he murmured, not moving forward. "Courage, my dear sister. It will be over soon."

Greatly relieved to see him, Catherine let out a slow breath. "And no one has entered?"

He shook his head. "None. Now, do hurry. I am sure Lord Winchester will not be far behind." He gave them both a warm smile, his eyes lingering on Catherine's before he stepped back to sit onto the window seat, the heavy gold-colored drapes falling back into place at once.

Turning towards Olivia, Catherine drew in a long breath, set her shoulders, and tried to smile. Olivia was clearly very anxious and was trembling slightly – something that Catherine could easily understand.

"You are going to do marvelously well," Catherine promised, grasping Olivia by the shoulders. "Remember, you are just to continue stating that you do not remember. That is all. I will appear to be very harsh with you, but you know why that is."

Olivia nodded. "I understand."

"Good."

They did not have any more time to talk for, just as Catherine stepped away from Olivia, the door opened and Lord Winchester swaggered in.

"Lord Winchester!" Olivia gasped, one hand flying to her mouth. "Whatever are you—?"

"Have you found it yet?" Lord Winchester interrupted harshly. "I know that you took it, Olivia. *You* know that you took it. Now is the time to declare yourself to be the thief and bring an end to this sham."

Catherine turned her eyes back to Olivia, planting her hands on her hips. "Lord Winchester has told me everything, Olivia. I know you must have taken the necklace from Lady Edgeware and then, in fright, hidden it in here."

"No," Olivia breathed. "I mean, I do not recall...." She trailed off, her skin milky white, as she let her eyes dart from Catherine back to Lord Winchester.

Delighted with Olivia's performance, Catherine shook her head sadly. "I know why you did it, of course. Your brother is a selfish man, is he not? He wants you to wed, but you have not found a suitor. He will cut you off, and you will have no other option but to become a companion or governess! How much you will have fallen, should that occur! It is understandable, Lady Olivia, but not an excuse. Now, tell me where you hid it, and perhaps I can help."

Lady Olivia drew in a long, shaking breath. "I do not remember that night at all," she stated, with a degree of firmness in her voice. "I do not think I took the necklace at all."

Lord Winchester let out a loud, mocking guffaw. "Of course you do not, Lady Olivia. Of course you do not remember taking the necklace and then hiding it from the rest of us!" He chuckled, shaking his head. "It will be in this room somewhere, I am certain of it."

Catherine let out another deep sigh, walking a little away from Olivia. "We must find it for you then. Shall we search the room, Lord Winchester? I am sure Lady Edgeware would be delighted if we retrieved it and, of course, you will be proven to be correct."

He grinned at her, clearly thrilled with the idea and the trust he believed her to be placing in him. "A capital idea, Miss Newton. Shall I start over here, near the door?" He directed his gaze towards Lady Olivia who was, by now, beginning to shake. "Perhaps you might sit down, Lady Olivia. You look as though you are about to collapse where you stand."

Catherine ignored Lady Olivia altogether, turning her back and beginning to search. She pulled aside cushions, opened drawers and generally made a meal of looking in places she knew would be empty. Minutes ticked by and her heart began to thunder in her chest, suddenly terrified that Lord Winchester would not do what she had hoped.

Only for him to cry out in delight.

Turning around, she saw Lord Winchester stand up tall from behind a blue velvet chaise longue, holding a sparkling ruby necklace in his fingers.

"It was hidden very securely, I must say, Lady Olivia," he said, grandly, as though declaring her guilt to all who would listen.

Catherine clapped her hands together, beaming at him whilst a huge wave of relief crashed over her. "Well done, Lord Winchester! Wherever did you find it?"

He chuckled and indicated a small wooden table in the corner which had a small drawer running along one side. "Right at the back of this drawer, on the opposite side," he said, walking towards Lady Olivia as the rubies caught the light. "Dear me, whatever shall we tell Lady Edgeware?"

At that very moment, the door opened, and Lady Edgeware walked in, followed closely by Lady Landerbelt and a rather strong looking footman.

"What do you have to tell me, Lord Winchester?" Lady Edgeware asked, arching one brow. "That you have found my ruby necklace?"

Catherine saw Lord Winchester pause for a moment, seemingly confused, before making an elegant bow and sweeping towards the lady.

"Indeed, I have, Lady Edgeware," he declared with a broad smile. "And I am afraid that Lady Olivia is now proven to be the guilty party." He glanced towards Catherine, his smile never faltering, but she did not return it.

Rather, she drew near to Lady Olivia and linked arms with her, drawing the lady close. She gave Lord Winchester a half smile as he frowned, clearly a little confused as to what was going on.

"Unlike you, Lord Winchester, I am less inclined to lay the blame at this girl's feet," Lady Edgeware murmured, as Lady Landerbelt stepped a little further into the room.

Lord Winchester frowned, as Lady Edgeware took the ruby necklace from him. "I do not quite understand what you mean, my lady."

Lady Edgeware glanced toward Lady Landerbelt, who nodded, a small smile on her face. Catherine felt a huge swell of relief crash over her as Lady Landerbelt called out, "You may come out now, Lord Caversham!"

Lord Winchester practically fell to the floor as the gold drapes were tugged aside and Lord Caversham came to stand by Olivia, one arm wrapped around her shoulders in a protective gesture.

"Lord Caversham," Lord Winchester spluttered. "I did not – I mean, you were not here when I entered, I..." He stuttered to a stop, his face now a little pale.

Catherine drew in a long breath, filled with satisfaction at seeing judgement done. She squeezed Lady Olivia's arm gently, seeing her friend's eyes fill with tears.

"What you do not understand, Lord Winchester, is that Lord Caversham has been here since the evening recital began,"

Catherine said in a loud voice. "He had to ensure that no one entered the room, other than myself and Lady Olivia."

Lord Winchester looked at her, confused. "And why would he need to ensure that?"

Lady Edgeware let out a small, harsh laugh. "To be certain that it could only have been you, Lord Winchester. I know it was you who stole my ruby necklace and then tried to place the blame on Lady Olivia, using your friend, Lord Dewford."

There was a moment of complete silence, and Catherine felt herself grow almost taut with tension. Lord Winchester was staring at Lady Edgeware, his mouth ajar, as though he could not believe what she was saying.

Either that, or he could not believe he had been discovered.

"You see, Lord Winchester, I knew that Lady Olivia was innocent," Lady Landerbelt began softly. "There was no reason for her to steal and, when her brother came to beg for my help, I felt I could do nothing less. In the course of my time with her, I have discovered that your brother, Henry, is the reason for your hatred of Lord Caversham and his sister."

Lord Winchester scoffed at once, although Catherine could see that a faint look of terror had drawn itself onto his expression. "Henry was a drunkard. He meant nothing to me."

"That is not so," Lord Caversham said, frowning. "He came to me in order to seek Olivia's hand in marriage, and I refused him. A short time later, he was pulled from the Thames. Using her influence and her connections, Lady Landerbelt has found out that you have never accepted the judgement of purposeful death. You have always sought to lay the blame elsewhere. In short, Lord Winchester, you blamed me."

"And that is why you tried to take everything from him," Catherine continued, as Lord Winchester began to stammer. "You thought to make his sister nothing more than a shadow of her former self, to have her gone from society and almost from the very world, just as you believed Lord Caversham to have done to your brother." She shook her head, her eyes lingering on Lord Winchester for a moment as she felt a modicum of sympathy and sadness for him. "It was shamefully done, Lord Winchester. And you are found out."

Lord Winchester drew in a long breath as two spots of red appeared on his cheeks. It seemed to Catherine that he realized he was out of luck, that he had nowhere to turn other than the truth.

"You used Lord Dewford's testimony to cast doubt on me," Lady Olivia said, haltingly. "And then Lord Darnley when it came to the pendant. You are a cruel, cruel man, Lord Winchester. You have caused me nothing but pain and misery, over something that was never my brother's fault."

"Lord Darnley told me everything," Lady Landerbelt said, as Lord Winchester opened his mouth apparently to deny this. "He had lost a great deal of money to you, had he?" She shook her head. "How easily you reigned him in, Lord Winchester. He aided you with Lady Olivia, in exchange for you forgetting about the debt he owed – oh yes, Lord Winchester you need not look so astonished. It is all going to come out now!"

Lord Winchester went puce, looking as if he might be violently sick right there in front of them all.

"And you need not try to claim as though someone else must have put the necklace where you found it," Lady Edgeware continued, a hard tone to her voice. "This is Beston, one of my footmen. He oversaw a complete search of this room earlier this afternoon. My husband and I were present. I can assure you that no necklace was found which means, Lord Winchester, you must have placed it there yourself."

"You are found out, Lord Winchester," Lady Olivia whispered, still trembling but yet with her chin held high. "*You* are the thief, and I will take the blame no longer."

Lord Winchester began to tremble from head to foot, his eyes turning onto Catherine with such fury that she felt herself shirk inside.

"You tricked me," he hissed, his hands curling into fists. "You told me—"

"I told you what you wanted to hear, Lord Winchester," Catherine replied firmly, determined to remain strong. "This is entirely your doing, and I will take no blame for it."

His angry gaze tore into Lord Caversham and, for a moment, Catherine thought Lord Winchester might attack the man.

"You took my brother from me," he shouted angrily, taking a step towards Lord Caversham, who moved protectively in front of his sister. "His death is on your head!"

Lord Caversham shook his head, his tone remaining steady and firm. "No, Lord Winchester, I take no blame. The death of your brother must have been truly terrible for you, but you did not need to pursue my sister with such ill intentions. Your grief has turned you cruel. This is over now. Finished. I suggest you remove yourself from town, Lord Winchester, just as soon as you are able." Stepping to one side, he offered his hand to Olivia. "Shall we, my dear?"

Olivia looked up into her brother's face, her expression finally relaxed and gentle. "Thank you, Caversham." Her gaze travelled past Lord Winchester towards Catherine and then to Lady Landerbelt. "Thank you both, for all you have done. This means more to me than I can ever truly express."

"You are more than welcome, my dear," Lady Landerbelt replied gently. "I am glad to have been able to restore your good name back to society at last."

Lady Edgeware turned towards Lord Winchester, as Catherine and Lady Landerbelt followed Lord Caversham and Lady Olivia out of the door.

"My husband will be seeing to you, Lord Winchester," she

said calmly. "Do remain here." She patted the footman's arm. "Beston will ensure you do so."

Lord Winchester began to shout frantically, but Lady Edgeware shut the door tightly behind them, a satisfactory smile on her face. Together, they all walked a little further along the hallway until Lord Winchester's voice could no longer be heard.

"My dear Lady Olivia," she murmured, stepping forward to take Olivia's hands. "I am truly sorry for all I have done that has wronged you. If you will permit me, I will take you now to the rest of the guests and declare the truth. The news will be all over town by morning."

Catherine smiled as Lady Olivia wiped her eyes with her lace handkerchief, before allowing Lady Edgeware and Lady Landerbelt to escort her back to the drawing room. That just left herself and Lord Caversham, who was looking at her with such a great sense of relief in his eyes that she could not help but go to him.

"My dear Catherine," Lord Caversham murmured, wrapping his arms around her waist. "You have done quite brilliantly, you know."

She sighed and rested her head against his chest for a moment, before looking up at him.

"It was mostly my aunt, as well you know," she said, smiling, "but I am glad for the part I was able to play. It was truly wonderful to see Olivia so happy."

He shook his head, as if unable to believe it was all over.

"And now I can think of new things," he said softly, looking down at her. "Catherine, you have become more dear to me than any other. I cannot bear the thought of being parted from you, not when my life is now finally unburdened. Do say that you will allow me to court you."

The sincerity and the eagerness in his eyes made her smile with joy, feeling as though all the happiness in the world had come to wrap itself around them both. "Caversham, I can think of nothing I would like more," she said softly. "I feel my heart crying out for you when we are apart, my mind caught up with nothing but thoughts of you. I love you, my dear Caversham, and will spend the rest of my days sharing my heart with you, if you will permit it."

It was a bold statement, she knew, but she did not regret saying it. Lord Caversham's eyes lit up at once, crushing her to him for a moment.

"I love you, Catherine," he whispered in her ear, his breath tickling across her cheek. "And I swear to you that I will have you by my side for the rest of my days, just as soon as I can arrange it." Letting her go just a little, he looked down at her with eyes that were filled with love. "Will that suit you, my dear?"

"Very much," she replied softly, before reaching up on her toes to press her lips to his. It was both a kiss and a promise of love, for today, for tomorrow, and for the rest of her life.

THE END

FREE EBOOK

Receive a FREE inspirational Regency Ebook by visiting our
website and signing up for our emailing list.
Click the link to enter www.HisEverLastingLove.com in your
web browser.

The newsletter will also provide information on upcoming new
books and new music.

THANK YOU!

Thank you so much for reading our book. We hope you
enjoyed it.

If you liked this book, we would really appreciate a five star
review on Amazon or Goodreads. Every review you take the
time to write makes an enormous impact on our writers' lives.
Reviews really encourage our authors and let them know the
positive things you enjoyed about their creativity.

Thank you again! I hope this book brightened your day.

ABOUT THE AUTHOR

Charlotte Fitzwilliam was raised in Manchester, England and graduated from University in London with a Masters of English, which focused on 18th Century and Romantic Studies. Her passion since young adulthood was reading and writing romantic regency stories.

Charlotte feels like she is living a dream life as she often brings coffee or tea to the country side. She sits beneath a tree with her laptop to dream and write about proud dukes and ladies in long dresses falling in love.